"And if I refuse to accept your money?"

Alex forced herself to meet Andros's eyes.

"Then I take the boy from you," he replied without hesitation.

He was serious but crazy, too, Alex decided. "You couldn't."

"As I said before, try me," he murmured. "I would sooner trade than go to court, but I shall if necessary, and with your past I shall win."

She had him, smug arrogant brute that he was. "And what if my past was solely a figment of your warped imagination?"

He laughed unpleasantly. "Academic, surely. Your only strength is being the boy's mother, but when I tell the courts you placed him in an orphanage, you will see a decision made, Miss Saunders—and it will be in *my* favor!"

Books by Alison Fraser

HARLEQUIN PRESENTS
697—PRINCESS
721—THE PRICE OF FREEDOM
745—COMING HOME

These books may be available at your local bookseller.

ALISON FRASER

coming home

Harlequin Books

TORONTO • NEW YORK • LONDON
AMSTERDAM • PARIS • SYDNEY • HAMBURG
STOCKHOLM • ATHENS • TOKYO • MILAN

Harlequin Presents first edition December 1984
ISBN 0-373-10745-5

Original hardcover edition published in 1984
by Mills & Boon Limited

CHAPTER ONE

'CAN I help you, madam?' the man behind the desk repeated, this time in *English*, a perceptive guess.

Could he help her? The faintly supercilious tone suggested not, and Alex, in faded jeans and travel-grubby blouse, frowned at it. She didn't need his doubts to add to her own.

Her gaze shifted sideways to the open lounge, a flight of steps lower than the entrance lobby, elegantly furnished and richly carpeted, and then back to the letter pigeonholes, row upon row of them on the other side of the reception desk. Wrong hotel? No! she dismissed staunchly; that didn't bear thinking about.

Although there was no one else waiting for his attention, the dark-suited clerk looked impatient at her hesitation.

'I have a reservation,' she returned stiffly.

'Name, please?' he reached for the register.

'Saunders, Alex,' she bristled, reading the obvious scepticism that took account of her casual, cheap clothing, and for good measure adding, 'Do you want me to spell it?'

But his eyes were already scanning the neatly typed list of expected arrivals before he declared, 'I'm afraid I have no rooms reserved in that name.'

His smile was not polite—it was satisfied.

Alex felt a moment's impulse to tell the Greek she would not stay in his stuck-up hotel even if he begged her to, but was, perhaps fortunately, distracted by the small hand tugging at her trouser leg.

'Lex?' the boy appealed.

He looked half asleep on his feet. To a six-year-old it must seem they had been travelling for days. She pushed the straggling black curls out of his eyes, murmuring, 'It's O.K., Nick,' and pulled him closer to lean on her leg. With renewed determination she addressed the clerk, 'Can you check again . . . please?'

His eyes barely glanced at his book before he shook his head. 'You must have the wrong hotel, madam.'

And wasn't he glad! Alex assessed angrily. Digging into her handbag, she smoothed a crumpled letter out on the desk.

'Is there another Apollo Hotel in Athens?' she asked, and to his reply of several, pursued anxiously, 'On a Charalambides Street?'

'No,' he admitted with reluctance.

So the hotel and street matched. Was Theo playing some sort of trick on them?—not a pleasant idea, but it sparked off another.

'The booking could have been made under a different name,' she suggested.

'Yes?' the clerk muttered shortly.

Alex drew in a breath and let it out on a less than hopeful, 'Kontos.'

She was prepared for a quick denial, a quietly worded request for her to leave—anything but his stunned look rapidly changing to alarm.

'Forgive me, Madame Saunderson, I am most sorry,' he apologised, his earlier cool replaced by instant humility.

'Saunders,' she corrected, dazed by the transformation, 'Miss.'

'I did not realise that . . .' he broke off nervously, and pushed forward his precious register, 'If you would like to sign the book, Miss Saunders.'

Recovering her spirits, Alex offered him a smile—it was more than satisfied. Then, head bent to write her name, she missed his discreet signal to a nearby porter and was also unaware of the man appearing in a doorway on the other side of the foyer.

'You wish to bring the guests to your office, *patron*?' the porter asked the man, anxious to please but careful to drain all curiosity from his voice.

'No, I don't think so,' the tall man next to him replied thoughtfully, a frown etching on his high forehead. 'She is not quite how I imagined ...' he said, more to himself than the hovering porter, whom he dismissed with a quiet, 'Thank you, Stavros.'

The man continued to study the girl as she crouched to pull up the boy's socks. No, she was not what he had expected from the brief description yielded by the enquiries made in London.

For blonde he had read platinum—not the honey-gold that fell, slightly tousled, to her shoulders. And she seemed younger than he had estimated she would be, younger than she could possibly be. The impression of youth was reinforced as she turned to follow a porter towards the lifts and he caught her full face for a moment.

Yet despite the plain, boyish clothes and his predisposition to dislike her on sight, he was struck by the girl's fair, fresh loveliness. Now why hadn't he expected that? He should have—had he forgotten Theo's weakness for a pretty face?

He cursed softly under his breath; he had allowed himself to be preoccupied with the woman, instead of the boy. Of him he had a photograph, good enough to intrigue, disturb even, but not conclusive. He should have used the opportunity to study the child carefully, guarding against the possibility of believing simply because he wanted it so.

He returned to his desk, and opened the top drawer. Taking out the letter and picture again, he looked long and hard at both—slim evidence, but somehow, instinct perhaps, he would *know* when he came face to face with the boy. He did not, however, relish this waiting; perhaps he should have tackled her straightaway. His doubts might have already been settled—one way or the other—if the woman's appearance had not stolen his attention.

Damn her!

The girl being damned that second stood just over the threshold of a room on the eleventh floor. To an outsider her stillness might have suggested she was overwhelmed by her surroundings, and admittedly the luxury had made a rather awesome impact.

But now she was gazing at the sun streaming through the wide balcony window, flooding the room with light—and thinking of the dingy basement rooms of their last flat; looking at the off-white silky wallpaper— but remembering other walls, peeling with damp; appraising the powder blue carpet and cream velour chairs—and contrasting them with the battered odds and ends their former landlord had considered furniture.

A mixture of anger and sadness was rising in her throat, threatening to make her cry out loud, but she swallowed it down. She saw that the boy too was finding their vastly-changed circumstances disturbing, his dark eyes darting round the room as though it was booby-trapped.

'What do you think, Nick?' She tilted his head towards hers and pulled a face. 'Could be worse, eh?'

He laughed, half understanding the humour.

'The chairs are white,' he announced in fascination.

'Nearly,' she nodded, then smiled at her thoughts. She'd give Nicky five minutes to remedy that situation! Or maybe ten—he wasn't a particularly messy child.

'Are we really staying here, Lex?' He was looking for reassurance.

'Well, we're here, aren't we?' she said brightly, but wondered how long it would be before someone arrived to give *her* reassurance. Still, if it turned out to be a nasty mistake—or worse, a bad joke—it would take no more than six months' dish-washing to pay for their night's accommodation, she thought wryly. They might as well use the room.

'Time you took a nap, I think,' she declared, catching Nicky fighting back a yawn.

'Aw no, Lex!' was the immediate reply.

'Aw yes, Nick,' she aped the ritualistic protest, and earned herself a grin. 'Come on, bed!'

As he was about to give in, the boy's grin suddenly widened. 'There isn't one, Lex.'

So there wasn't. She had been too busy taking in the room as a whole to spot that obvious detail. Good grief, they must be occupying a suite!

Suitcase in one hand and Nicky in the other, she opened the second door in the room and walked into a bedroom. As plush as the sitting room, she amended her estimate of enforced labour to a year, and almost laughed. Or was it a touch of hysteria?

Helping Nicky out of his tee-shirt and shorts, clammily sticking to his body, she folded them back in their suitcase. When she made to tuck Nicky between the cool cotton sheets, her thoughts were less humorous ... skinny, sickly, beautiful child that he was. The hollows of his cheeks had become suspiciously damp.

'What's wrong, Nick?'

He rubbed the back of his hand over his eyes in an attempt to hide and halt the flow of tears. Impossibly stoical boy child—and who had made him that way? she mused guiltily.

'He never came,' he whispered, trapping a sob in the back of his throat.

Oh, Chris, Alex despaired once more, why did you tell him? Why did you let him believe—and then leave us, needing you?

'Why, Lex?' He was waiting, trusting, gazing up at her as if she were the fountain of all knowledge.

It served her right—for that bright, breezy, lying confidence she had been sustaining throughout the last days. She was a sham!

'Remember all those cars on the road from the airport?' she said now. 'Well, he probably got stuck in a traffic jam. Just think, he might have passed us.'

Sham!—just think of all the other possibilities—like his having changed his mind since making the hotel booking, forgotten us again as he had for the last three years.

But apparently she wasn't the only one beginning to have doubts, for Nicky asked rather starkly, 'What if he *doesn't* come?'

'Then we'll go back to London and . . .'

'Not to that place, Lex . . . Not to that place!' he interrupted fretfully.

He didn't have to explain the fear he felt to Alex, but it affected her so deeply, she found herself saying, 'No, never again, Nick. That was a mistake.'

'Promise,' he pressed.

'Cross my heart . . .' she started, but stopped herself in time from adding the usual 'and hope to die'. Nicky didn't seem to notice the near-slip as he gave her a hard, forceful hug, sealing the bargain. His grieving period had been intense but short; she wished it could be the same for her . . . 'Now go to sleep, Nicky, and we'll go for a walk later.'

When he finally drifted off, Alex lay on her back on the other twin bed, listening to his breathing—overwhelmed by the commitment she'd made. There was no going back on it; somehow a promise to a child was even more irrevocable than to an adult. And she didn't want to—he was hers now, unless Theo claimed him.

But what if she was forced to break it? Become just another disappointment to a child too used to them. Have again to stand back helpless when they took him away from her.

They hadn't been cruel about it. Surely she could see it was for the best, they'd reasoned. She was a little young, not yet twenty-one. And yes, they understood why she and her sister had deceived their landlord, but unfortunately he had the right to refuse renewal of the lease if the 'no children' clause had been violated. Perhaps in time they could review the situation.

But it had been a very vague 'perhaps' and their eyes hadn't held out much hope for her plans. Even if she'd got her language degree, good jobs were elusive; even without a child, good flats were like gold dust.

To allay her fears, they had shown her round the children's home. Not a bad place—a haven for abused and unloved children. But the large, noise-filled rooms had been too familiar—a hell for children with quiet ways and loving backgrounds, like Nicky ... like herself twelve years earlier.

Only she'd had Chris, her big sister, to make their Home more of a purgatory where they ate and slept, talked of happy times before their parents' accident and waited for future dreams, endlessly discussed, to come true. And Nicky would have no one.

So she'd pleaded with them. They'd given her a few days, but they ran out too quickly, and with them, her hope. Then they'd taken Nicky.

By that time Alex had all but forgotten the letter Chris had written just before she had gone into hospital—Chris still believing in her handsome Greek husband.

They had met on the same hotel management course, fallen head over heels in love, married and had Nicky within the year. On Alex's sixteenth birthday Chris had come back for her, and she had been as grateful as a puppy rescued from Battersea, made welcome and wanted in her new home, but never quite trusting that such happiness could last.

It hadn't. Three years ago Theo had made his annual trip to see his family in Greece, and hadn't come back. Their letters had gone unanswered. Alex had worried with Chris, and wept with her, and then tried to share her faith that any day, any hour, any minute, he would be back to make things perfect again.

After a year it seemed Chris too had given up. They had moved to a cheaper flat, one in a succession. Insisting Alex stay at university, Chris had taken a job as a hotel receptionist, working nights so one of them was always with Nicky.

They had managed somehow, even after Chris's dizzy spells had started. Alex was days off finishing college and she would be able to look after them all while Chris had the rest she needed. But time had cheated her of the chance. Chris's anaemia had turned out to be a serious blood disease. She had hung on for Alex's sake and then faded back to memories, until she had slipped away from them altogether. Her death had left Alex believing in little, least of all the possibility of a reply to her sister's last desperate show of faith.

And even now, as the sound of Nicky stirring restlessly in his sleep brought her back to the present, she still questioned it—why had he bothered after all this time?

Too strung up to sleep, she rose from the bed and wandered out on to the balcony. It was enclosed on both sides by a striped canopy, ensuring absolute privacy. Leaning on the wall, she peered down at the smart streets below, reminiscent of Knightsbridge, trying to make some sense of it all—Theo's letter, stiff and formal and so unlike the laughing young man she had once liked so much, and this luxurious hotel, surely beyond Theo's means. But any explanations she came up with, she didn't want to be true.

A faint cry brought her in from the balcony to find Nicky awake, his eyes wide with apprehension. Kneeling down on the bedcover, she stroked the hair back from his heated face.

'I'm here,' she whispered, sensing he was in the confused state between sleeping and waking, alarmed at their strange surroundings.

'Thought I was alone,' he mumbled, voice thick with drowsiness. As he pulled himself up on the pillows, his expression became more alert. 'Has he come?'

'Not yet,' she murmured soothingly, and quickly added, 'How about taking me for a walk?'

'Where, Lex?'

'There's a park nearby. You can see it from the window,' she told him, taking fresh clothes out of the suitcase. 'I think you need a wash first, though, don't you?'

'No,' he shook his head gravely but gave a heartening

laugh when Alex half dragged, half tickled him in the direction of the bathroom.

'The taps are gold, Lex,' he declared when she kneeled him on a stool next to the wash-hand basin.

'I wouldn't be at all surprised,' she murmured wryly before ordering, 'Now stop squirming! You know you love it,' and cutting off his protests with a fresh attack of the wet flannel on his grubby face. Then flicking a comb through his hair, she announced, 'There, almost human,' which made him giggle, at ease and open with the most important person in his world. 'Now scoot and get dressed while I do something about myself—I look as though I've been pulled through a hedge backwards!'

The boy screwed up his face at the unfamiliar expression before passing on the shy confidence, 'Billy Simons thinks you're beautiful, Lex,' and left his aunt laughing softly at her reflection and the admiration it had evoked from another six-year-old.

Alex would have been a fool not to know she was attractive, but she took no great pride in her looks. The young college men rash enough to flatter them had been rebuffed with a few well-chosen flippancies. The more secure had laughed, but others had labelled her hard for her seemingly careless rejection. Indifferent, Alex had breezed through college life with an air of confidence that was, in part, quite real. And if anyone had suggested that her attitude was coloured with a fear of involvement, they would have received a derisive laugh for their trouble.

God, but she was out of her element! Alex decided as the lift descended.

'See the clock, Lex—does that mean there really are thirty floors?'

'Yes, Nick,' she answered briefly, conscious of the curious stares of the elegantly dressed couple sharing the lift.

She imagined them to be disdainful until Nicky piped

up, 'Is it a skyscratcher, then?' and they laughed with her.

'Skyscraper,' she corrected with a smile.

'What's the difference?' Nicky pursued, now in a stage whisper, for he was shy of the two strangers.

But when Alex didn't find an immediate answer the woman, an American, laughed, 'I think he's got you there. Cute little feller.'

'Yes,' Alex acknowledged the woman's friendliness. So much for her paranoia, she reprimanded herself as they stepped out of the lift.

Before they could reach the street doors, however, they were detained by the desk clerk who, on being informed of their intention to go for a walk in the park, began to stress the size of Athens and its labyrinth of streets. His dire warnings seemed ridiculous to Alex, who had been born and bred in London. She looked askance at the fingers that held her arm, and he hastily dropped his hand, although his protests followed her to the door.

In fact the park proved remarkably simple to locate, and she took careful note of the street names and shops they passed en route. It was laid out with gentle sloping stretches of grass through which pebblestone paths had been cut, but the vegetation was more exotic than in London parks. Plants that were strictly of the house 'pampered' variety at home grew rampant in the fierce Mediterranean heat.

Nicky skipped ahead of her until they reached a fountained water basin, bordered by statues Alex suspected were *modern* 'Ancient Grecian' even if they had the requisite missing limbs. Nicky stared with unabashed curiosity, but Alex found the nude figures, sculpted with a painstaking dedication to detail, more than a little embarrassing. She would never, of course, have admitted it, for that near-shyness shot some rather gaping holes in her blasé front.

Aimlessly they headed away from the entrance further into the park where it was shaded and quieter, the paths hedged by tall flowering shrubs, and Alex was concentrating on the peace and beauty rather than the isolation of their surroundings when they came upon some youths gathered in a clearing just ahead of them.

Nicky spotted them first with, 'Funny boys, Lex!'

Normally she would have laughed at the description he reserved for skinheads and punk rockers alike, and at the notion that Britain was still a world leader in certain respects, even if it was in the export of dubious trends of fashion. Indeed the motley crew looked a lot less intimidating that their British counterparts, although they fell silent at their approach.

Later she was to wonder if that had been her mistake—hesitating and then retreating instead of walking straight through their ranks.

It wasn't until they had recovered a hundred yards of the path they had just walked that Alex became fully conscious that they were being shadowed by some of the young men. With a cursory glance behind her to confirm her impression, she continued on, increasing her pace.

They too lengthened their stride, their voices growing chillingly louder, the shouts to attract her attention quickening the beat of her heart. Knowing that on a logical level it would prove an idiotic move, she was unable to curb her instinct to run. Snatching Nicky's hand tighter, she took to her heels, the sound of hurrying footsteps—hers? theirs? hers?—spacing the beats between the rhythmic pounding in her eardrums.

'Dear God, not with Nicky here!' was her last silent prayer as she saved the boy from falling and then ran blindly into a solid object in her path. Was it her startled terrified cry that rent the air as firm hands reached out to steady and take the impact of her hurtling body?

Snapping back her head, she took in a pair of frigidly cold eyes, so dark they appeared black, and she had to stifle another scream that rose in her throat. She could have imagined no man further apart from one of

Nicky's 'funny' boys, yet for a moment she was just as frightened of her saviour, with his striking similarity to the statues lining the water fountains. And then she recovered sufficiently from the impact to know she should be thanking him, but the words wouldn't come as she looked up at his immobile implacable countenance. The face with its chiselled high-boned angularity was too perfect, unreal, and the long straight nose and the slight curve of his lips stamped it with an arrogance from which her mind automatically recoiled.

Suddenly aware that he still had a hold on her, Alex pulled herself away, breasts rising and falling in the effort to regain her breath. Embarrassed by his steady gaze, she stepped back a pace, glancing over her shoulder. Her would-be assailants had disappeared into thin air, on catching sight of the older man.

When she turned back, she was still the object of his cold silent scrutiny. There was something in the way his appraising eyes travelled over her slim body that was almost more alarming than the threat from the youths. She felt, however ridiculous, that she had been thoroughly undressed for his clinical inspection, and now even the intention of expressing her gratitude, failed her.

Then his eyes moved sideways to Nicky and stayed on the boy, losing their coldness. Nicky was panting and coughing slightly, but although he had one hand fisting the cloth of Alex's trousers, he returned the man's interest with more fascination than fear.

The man said something in Greek, directed at Nicky. Too low and guttural for Alex to interpret, and of course, Nicky looked totally blank.

'I'm afraid he doesn't understand. We're English,' Alex explained, hoping he would understand her so that she would not have to resort to her inadequate command of his language. She imagined he did from his eyes narrowing on Nicky's black hair and Mediterranean complexion.

'Really?' he replied laconically.

Disbelievingly perhaps? At any rate, it prompted Alex to assert, 'Yes, both of us,' and realising an innocent contradiction might come from another quarter, touched her nephew's shoulder. 'Nick, go and sit on that bench over there for a minute.'

'But . . .'

'Now!' she urged, pushing him in the right direction, since he seemed oddly reluctant to detach his eyes from the man's, which followed him to the bench before flicking back to Alex. Cold again, but disturbing all the same. She wasn't aware of betraying her nervousness till he spoke.

'*I* am not going to harm you,' he told her in faultless English, cultured and only slightly accented.

His smooth manner should have calmed her, but instead her stomach tightened with an emotion that was close to anger. Her reply, forced through dry lips, surprised even Alex.

'I didn't for one moment believe you were.'

His jaw clenched perceptibly at her tone.

'Indeed?' he responded, an edge creeping into his voice. 'For a woman who was in grave danger of being raped, you appear to be taking it very calmly.'

'I wasn't!' she snapped back, reacting to his bluntness.

'Taking it calmly?' he countered.

'In danger of being r . . . robbed,' she amended hastily, and was subjected to another of his slow, demeaning appraisals.

'No, I am sure you were in no danger of being . . . robbed,' he drawled in purposeful agreement. His eyes switched pointedly to a clump of low vegetation and then back to her face. 'They had much more interesting plans for you.'

The suggestiveness of the lazy accented voice triggered the rash claim, 'I can take care of myself,' from an Alex, growing defiantly angry. She realised what he was trying to do: intimidate her with his superior height, teach her a lesson on how thoughtless she had been veering from the main park area. Well, it was already learned, and she didn't need his overbearing attitude to drum it home.

When she failed to back away or drop her eyes from his, he announced in abrupt biting tones, 'Women in this country recognise and admit to their limitations. You would do well to follow their example, English girl.'

Intended to conclude the matter, it served only to stir Alex further.

'No doubt limitations reinforced by the arrogant Greek male desperately clinging on to a Stone Age mentality,' she retaliated—but as the words echoed in her own mind, she knew, without the fury pulsing a beat at his temple, that she had gone too far. On the verge of retracting, she was denied the opportunity.

'Perhaps I have cheated you out of an adventure, madame. From your attitude I can only deduce that I have misinterpreted the situation ... that the young men were merely following where you led ...'

Her hand struck of its own volition, full force on his left cheek, and wiped away his sneer.

His desire to hit her back was nearly tangible as she stared up at him, in shock at her own violence. It was betrayed in the eyes burning down into hers, just as the force of will holding him back was revealed by the sheer immobility of his features.

What saved her? she later wondered—an exercise of extreme control or Nicky suddenly appearing to thrust his small body between them?

'Leave Lex 'lone!' he cried, reverting to baby diction in his excitement. His body pressed back into hers, Alex sensed rather than witnessed his glaring up at the stranger, but it was the man's reaction, the instant change in him, that left her gaping.

He smiled.

'For you, young man, yes,' he agreed. Then to her he muttered in a low undertone, pitched well above the child's head, 'One day I shall make you very sorry you did that, woman!'

As she watched his retreating figure, Alex found herself shivering—at her own uncontrolled flare of anger; at the quiet intensity of his threat.

'He looked like one of the stone men, 'cept with his clothes on,' Nicky declared, seeking her confirmation. Remarkably the face upturned to hers was wondering rather than frightened.

'Didn't he, Lex?'

'Yes . . . yes, he did,' she reluctantly admitted to the Greek commanding presence. But despite the expensive lounge suit he had been wearing and his polished, clipped English, he had seemed for that tense suspended moment—Alex searched for the word to fit and found—uncivilised.

'He was awfully angry when you hit him,' Nicky gave his own version, evidently fascinated by the man.

'Let's go back.' Her unusual sharpness stemmed any more questions from the six-year-old and with a mental shrug she decided to dismiss the whole incident as quickly as possible.

There was no sign of the youths, but she still made a hurried exit that directly contradicted her bold confidence in her ability to defend herself, and she was relieved there was no one around, except Nicky, to witness it.

In that she was mistaken. He had headed straight for the gate, impatiently turned back thirty yards from it, then waited and watched from a discreet distance till they were clear of the park, although in spirit he felt himself at the other end of the spectrum from a guardian angel.

He had never wanted to hit a woman in his life before, but he had come close to slapping the damn woman, and maybe he would be feeling a great deal better now if he had given way to the impulse. As he recalled her derisive 'Stone Age mentality', his mouth went into an even tighter line—an insult to a country whose people had once initiated one of the greatest civilisations in the world when her ancestors had been little more than cave-dwellers. It was natural that he should repay the insult, but he hadn't anticipated her response.

No, she wasn't what he had expected (some brassy giggling blonde), she was a damn sight worse, with her insolent blue eyes and her impudently pouting mouth; daring to slap him and having the nerve to face up to him afterwards.

But the child—oh yes, he was all he could have hoped for, and more. Pale and too thin by far, yet so like Theopolis as a boy that he had claimed him right then and there, only to have the woman disclaim the boy's Greek origins. Not that she had understood, and now he was glad she hadn't, because he was not a man who liked his emotions on show. Next time he would be ready for her . . .

Make her very sorry, would he? Alex repeated sulkily to herself, while Nicky tucked into the food she had ordered. Surely an idle threat, for all its forceful delivery. What were the chances of them ever meeting again? A million to one in a city this size? More? Whatever, she reassured herself in her ignorance, with odds that stretched towards impossibility.

But part of her wanted a replay in which she didn't lose her head, or slap his arrogant face. For she might not have backed down when she could have, but Alex Saunders had no taste for scenes, and although she apportioned the blame largely on him, she could not quite forgive herself for that sweeping remark about Greek males. It was on a par with believing all Australians swilled beer in between vulgar conversation or expecting Americans to have loud voices and even louder dress sense. Both stupid, narrow-minded prejudices and as absurd as the image of the British going around with perpetual stiff upper lips. No, she wasn't very proud of that piece of irrationality.

After all, the only other Greek she had met was Theo, and not once in the two years she had lived with them had she ever seen him anything but kind and lighthearted, and almost reverential in his loving of Chris.

That was what had made his defection so hard to take—no cross words exchanged, no ripple on the surface of their marriage. Sometimes she wondered if there were things Chris hadn't told her . . . well, in a few hours she would know.

The receptionist had telephoned a message left by Theo, asking her to meet him in the cocktail bar downstairs at eight. She didn't much like the venue of their meeting, but it was better than his coming up to the suite. For Nick to waken and recognise his father, only to be rejected by him in the long run, would be too cruel.

Alex called room service to remove the remains of their meal and settled Nicky down with some of the play books she had bought for the journey. She needed time to think. . . .

It had come out when she tried to tell him about the Home, which was no longer a threat but an inevitability. 'Listen to me, Nicky,' she started falteringly, an hour before his bedtime. 'You're going away for a little while to a new home,' but her tongue stuck on any platitudes she could have uttered and he had interrupted her before she could explain.

'Yes, I know,' he said with a bright clarity, 'Mummy told me.'

'Mummy told you?' Alex echoed, astonished, and while he nodded firmly, she quickly concluded that whatever Mummy had told him was certainly not the piece of news she was trying to impart. 'What, Nick?'

'That we'd be going away, 'course,' he repeated what Alex had said, with a frown for her slowness.

A nasty sinking feeling entered her stomach. 'Where, Nick? Where did Mummy tell you?' and turned it over when he answered, 'To Greece—to see Daddy.'

Lord, how could Chris have? she moaned silently, but

it was not an accusation, more a plea for her help. She searched for the right words to account for his mother's confused state in the last weeks.

'Nicky, when you go to sleep,' she murmured tentatively, 'do you ever imagine you're someone else— say a cowboy?'

'Spaceman,' he corrected.

'Well, in the same sort of way, Mummy used to imagine living in Greece because it would be warm and sunny and not as noisy as London, but it was just like your wishing to be a spaceman,' she explained, while his dark eyes held hers. 'Just a dream,' she concluded sadly.

For answer Nicky climbed down from his chair, half carried, half dragged it over to a rickety bookshelf in one corner, and placed it squarely on the floor. Before she could help him, he had stood on the chair and picked out the book he wanted.

The atlas looked ancient, badly scarred by damp, but it took him a couple of seconds to find his page.

'That's where, Lex.' A small finger completely obscured a tiny dot in the Mediterranean, just one of a series of tiny islands off the mainland. 'If it was a dream, it wouldn't be on the map, would it?' he appealed to her, and made Alex wish she had never started the conversation.

She should have disillusioned him; instead she said, 'I think it's time you went to bed, Nicky.'

But he was not to be so easily sidetracked.

'When can we go, Lex?'

'Not at the moment, Nick.'

'When?'

Sometime, never. She had to tell him. 'We'll see,' she found herself saying—joining the ranks of all the adults who had told her temporising lies when she had first lost her parents.

The next morning she had told him about the children's home. As best she could—which turned out to be badly. He hadn't understood much. Alex had left him at the door with the superintendent, and the look of recrimination he cast at her as she waved goodbye had wounded more deeply than any words of betrayal.

Then, two days later, the letter arrived. She stared at the Greek stamp in disbelief, read its contents over and over till the words sank in.

'Received Chris's letter. No matter what happened in the past, I would like you to bring my son to Greece. I have had deposited some money in your name at the Bank of Athens, London—an initial sum for your expenses. Telegraph the Apollo Hotel, Charalambides Street, Athens, the date of your arrival. A room will be reserved for you.

Have no doubts I am interested in the boy's welfare.

Theo.'

But she didn't rush to the Bank of Athens. And despite Theo's instruction, the formal tone of the typed letter alone made her uneasy. She wasn't sure what she would have done about it if Nicky hadn't precipitated a decision.

When she opened the door the following evening to an agitated Miss Turner, she summed up the situation at a glance.

'He's wandered?' She didn't really need to ask the question; she knew.

'Hasn't been seen since school,' the social worker informed her quickly. 'We'd hoped he'd come back to you.'

'I'll get my jacket.' Alex's voice acquired a distracted note as the years fell away. She had done her own share of wandering in the beginning. 'Have you tried the park?—the one near the house?'

'No, I came here first,' Miss Turner replied. 'Why, do you think . . .'

'Just a guess,' Alex said defensively, reluctant to admit her reasoning—that it had been one of her refuges. 'We have to start somewhere.'

So they started at the small pond, giving his description to other children and getting mostly negative or confused answers, moved on to the swing area with no success, and finally covered every inch of the park until Miss Turner was more than ready to collapse on the nearest bench.

'I'm sorry,' Alex muttered, at last noticing the older woman's laboured breathing.

'No, it's ... it's all right,' the other gasped, well satisfied that Alex's frantic pace was a measure of her caring. When she regained her breath, she asked quietly, 'So where else did *you* used to go?'

Alex darted her a hostile glance. 'What do you mean?'

'We had to look into your background,' Miss Turner revealed, 'but I'd already half guessed.'

'Shows, does it?' Alex muttered rather acidly, but was grateful when Pamela Turner let it pass. She had come to like the woman. 'Is it going to make a difference to my having Nicky back? Truthfully?'

'Truthfully—maybe,' Miss Turner admitted regretfully. 'Although you're the boy's aunt, in ways it's treated the same as adoption. Your lack of family backing is a disadvantage.'

Alex absorbed it in a long moment of silence before saying impulsively, 'What if I can produce a father?'

Miss Turner frowned. 'I didn't realise you were ... er ... engaged,' she replied uncertainly, although the apparent absence of a boy-friend had surprised her. Alex Saunders was a very good-looking girl.

'I'm not.' Alex drew the letter from her back pocket and handed it over. She registered Miss Turner's surprise; she was not the only one who had regarded Nicky's father as a lost cause. She pressed, 'Does that make a difference?'

'I'm not sure—probably,' Miss Turner replied cautiously. 'Let's talk about it later, mm?'

And they had, after they followed another of Alex's hunches and found Nicky in the borough library, tucked in a corner of the children's section.

Alex sat down quietly at his side to whisper, 'Talking to me, kiddo?'

He answered it with one of his fierce hugs, head ramming into her shoulder, and then with a suspicion of a sniff, said, 'It's disappeared, Lex.'

Alex looked down at the page of the junior atlas, too basic to show every dot in the Mediterranean, back at the mute appeal in his sad dark eyes, and hugged him hard again so he wouldn't see the tears flowing helplessly from her eyes.

But Pamela Turner saw them. And maybe ... probably ... positively, they had moved her to stick her neck out, cut red tape and allow them to leave five days later on a Greece-bound jet.

CHAPTER TWO

THE hotel babysitter came at fifteen minutes to the hour, and Alex was as ready as she would ever be. She had changed into a light cotton jumpsuit, fawn in colour and drawn at the ankles—last year's fashion and her best. Glancing in the mirrored tiles of the bathroom, she flicked her hair out from its stand-up collar and decided it would have to do. In fact, fashionable or not, the simple outfit enhanced her fairness and slender figure.

Downstairs, a sweeping glance at the cocktail bar told her Theo had not matched her early arrival, and she allowed a waiter to guide her to one of the quieter booths in the rear.

In passable Greek she ordered a glass of white wine and searched her bag for a cigarette. A lighter flicked a few inches from her face as she looked in vain for matches, and raising her head, she expected to see Theo Kontos. The man was young and dark and Greek, but there the similarity ended.

She accepted the light with a slight smile, but when the young man pursued it with a request to sit down, she firmly shook her head. Undiscouraged, he bounced back with a trite remark about their both being alone and an even more inane comment Alex loosely translated as the Greek version of the night being young.

It left her between laughter and annoyance, and she was fruitlessly scanning her limited Greek vocabulary for the equivalent of 'buzz off' when it was supplied for her.

She didn't have to move her head round to identify the owner of the deep masculine voice which continued in English, 'You don't waste any time, do you?'

'What?' Alex frowned as she watched the younger man rapidly retreat.

'Forget it,' he cancelled his remark—but too late. Alex had read the flicker of contempt that had accompanied it before he himself sat at her table, uninvited.

'On the contrary,' she reacted to his insinuation, 'your countrymen are just living up to their reputation for amorousness. Without much finesse, I might add.'

'Really?' he responded coldly.

'Yes, *really*. The hot weather, I suppose,' she trotted out the silly prejudice with a condescending air.

'Meaning?' he challenged, unnecessarily, Alex was sure.

She awarded herself a point before echoing him with an airy, 'Oh, forget it.'

'Are you trying to be clever, Miss Saunders?' he muttered incisively.

'*Trying?* . . . no,' she responded, but her bland smile for the dark look he shot her almost said—succeeding, yes. And she was so busy giving herself a mental pat on the head, she completely missed his use of her surname.

'I would like to talk to you,' he announced with visible restraint, and before she could speak, qualified it with, 'Preferably without trading insults.'

She moved her studied concentration from the tip of her cigarette back to his face and then his eyes. They were as cold as his voice—little wonder this man resented being classed a hot-blooded Mediterranean!

'I can't think why, unless it's to carry out your big bad threat of this afternoon,' she replied with a bored drawl. She let her eyes skirt round the bar, filling up with pre-dinner drinkers. 'Bit crowded, wouldn't you say?'

For a long moment he didn't *say* anything; simply stared at her in a coldly analytical way that had her looking away first.

Then in a carefully measured tone he told her, 'I think it might be better if we forget this afternoon also, if we are to have a rational discussion. You may assume I regret any remarks of a personal nature I might have made.'

Alex could have taken his about-face as an apology. She didn't. The way it was phrased smacked of appeasement, nothing more. Why?

'As long as you don't expect me to reciprocate,' she countered suspiciously.

'I wouldn't be that ambitious,' he laughed without humour.

'Good. Now at the risk of adding to my tarnished image, may *I* say that I'm waiting for a man to join me.' She stubbed out her cigarette, a dismissive gesture. 'And you can definitely assume you will be superfluous to any discussion, rational or otherwise. So if you don't mind, Mr . . .' she trailed off with heavy indifference.

'Perhaps I'd better introduce myself,' he murmured as though he hadn't heard it, and when Alex was least ready for it, supplied with deliberate understatement, 'Kontos . . . Andros Kontos—Theo's brother.'

And then he waited, anticipated . . .

Anything but Alex's appearance of calm, entirely superficial, as her features remained rigid while her mind scrabbled for an appreciation of what he had just said.

Why should a total stranger tell her he was Theo's brother, if it wasn't true? She couldn't find a reason, yet she didn't want to believe it. She brought his proud angular face back into focus and refused to see anything of Theo in the hard, unyielding countenance.

On a note of rejection she finally said, 'You claim to be Theo's brother?'

'I am afraid it is you who *claims* to be something to Theo, *Miss* Saunders,' he matched her cool . . . just. 'I *know* I am Theo's brother.' He went into the top pocket of his jacket and impatiently threw its contents on the table in front of her.

Before she opened the passport, Alex knew it would, of course, prove he was who he had said. But she did it all the same, partially to gain time to recover her wits and perhaps because she guessed it would displease him.

She was right. Andros Nikolas Kontos was an important man, had been for over fifteen of the thirty-seven years claimed by the birth date in his passport. He was not used to his word being doubted, least of all by a slip of an English girl who possessed a self-assurance more irritating than any show of dramatics he had been half expecting.

'Where's Theo?' she asked bluntly.

He avoided it with, 'I am here to negotiate on his behalf. That's all you need to know.' He slipped the passport back into his jacket and continued briskly, 'I have seen the boy and am prepared to accept at face value that he is my brother's child.'

'Who the hell else's could he be?' Alex rapped out angrily. 'And believe me, the fact of it has brought damn little pleasure over the last few years, and no more so than this exact moment!'

'So I gathered.'

The quiet comment with its derisive edge jarred Alex's nerves further. So he gathered what? Undoubtedly both more and less than he should. What slanted version had he heard from his younger brother? Whatever it was she decided she would sooner talk to Theo.

She caught him off guard by rising so abruptly, but he intercepted her before she had taken more than a couple of paces towards the exit. The hand curled round her arm held her fast and she wheeled round.

'I won't deal with you—understand!' she spat out.

His grip tightened. 'You have no choice.'

'Haven't I?' Her voice was as cutting as the look she directed at the long brown fingers forcing her to stand still. Switching her eyes back to his, she threatened, 'In exactly thirty seconds I shall call over the waiter who's staring so avidly at us and tell him you're molesting me. Do you want a scene?'

His sharp glance at the young waiter indeed watching them implied that he didn't, but neither did he make any move to release her arm.

'I wouldn't do that if I were you,' he suggested smoothly—too smoothly for Alex's liking. 'The young man wouldn't know how to handle the situation and I just might have to sack him for trying to ... Understand?'

She was beginning to; the waiter had occupied himself elsewhere the second Kontos had glanced at him.

'You manage the hotel,' she deduced with a frown.

He shook his head, noted her small sigh of relief and then corrected drily, 'I *own* the hotel.'

And wasn't he enjoying delivering that piece of information! Alex fumed as it sank in.

'All the more reason you wouldn't like a scene, I would have thought,' she rallied.

'Maybe,' he agreed urbanely—then smiled, or what Alex assumed passed for this man's smile. 'However, I assure you that any embarrassment will be all yours, Miss Saunders.'

Alex just bet it would. The man was on his home ground and prepared to use any power it gave him. He must have been reading her mind, for he suddenly released her arms as though his hold was no longer necessary.

'Do you like your suite, Miss Saunders?' he continued in an undertone. 'It's one of our best.'

'You wouldn't!' she gasped, one step ahead of his bland enquiry.

'Try me,' he murmured. The travesty of a smile returned. Now they understood each other perfectly, but he drove the point home. 'Perhaps I should warn you that it is rather late to find other accommodation if you're not satisfied ...'

He would! And for late substitute impossible.

'Message received loud and clear, Mr Kontos,' she muttered flippantly. 'Nevertheless I'd still like to see

Theo, even if he hasn't the guts to do his own negotiating, as you term it.'

A spasm of some dark emotion flickered into his eyes, shading them black, then she found herself being whisked through a side door and down a long empty corridor to the rear of the hotel. Andros's fingers slid away from her arm as he went to unlock what was obviously a private lift.

'Where are we going?' she demanded.

'My quarters,' he replied flatly, expecting her to follow him into the lift.

'To see Theo?' It was more a delay than a question, because suddenly she was nervous of him, nervous of getting into the small five-foot square with him. No concrete reason, she just was.

'What's wrong?' he asked, ignoring her question and obviously impatient at her hesitation.

'I ... I don't like confined spaces,' Alex invented lamely.

'It takes approximately thirty seconds to reach the penthouse,' he informed her with a factual air.

It made Alex feel foolish, probably his intention. What was she nervous about?—that he'd go off his cool head and pounce? Now that was ridiculous, she scorned the idea. A man less interested in her attractions and more contemptuous of herself, she had yet to meet. She forced herself to step into the lift.

'You'll be quite safe,' he assured her, flicking her a glance. She had positioned herself in the farthest corner from him. It half amused, half irritated him. 'Provided you can manage to keep your opinions to yourself for thirty seconds, that is,' he added, as he closed the lift door on them.

Alex opened her mouth at his softly spoken mockery, only to clamp it shut again. She tilted her head back and her face once more became a study in defiance.

'You seem to have recovered your nerve,' Andros Kontos observed, suddenly turning to catch that haughty insolence so quickly back in place.

The lift had stopped, but he was in no hurry to open the door. His regard was calculating. If she'd really been claustrophobic, between his towering presence and the lack of breathing space, she would be hysterical by now and clamouring to get out. They both knew it.

'No answer, Miss Saunders?' he jibed, voice sounding deep and hollow in the enclosed lift.

'I'm keeping my opinions to myself, as instructed,' Alex returned tartly.

'Long may it last,' he murmured under his breath as he at last pressed the open button and she moved, stiff-backed, past him.

Alex pretended not to hear. In fact she had every intention of ignoring him entirely the moment Theo appeared.

The lift led directly into a lounge, but its steel door was not out of place. Furnished predominantly in blacks and greys with only a smattering of brighter red for contrast, if the room was luxurious, it was also uncompromisingly functional. Expensive hi-fi ranged against one wall, a well stocked bar against another, with a suite of the finest black leather in the central living area, but nothing that couldn't be put to practical use—no ornaments or photographs or even pictures. Its stark colour scheme and economical lines lacked warmth—the room reflected its owner.

It was also empty, apart from the two of them.

'Where's Theo?' Alex demanded.

'Would you like a drink?' Andros went over to the bar and placed two glasses on its dark wood surface. She stubbornly reiterated her question, and he looked up from pouring himself a brandy and suggested she should sit down.

'He's not here, is he?' she challenged, gave him adequate time to deny it, then started towards the lift.

He halted her with an abrupt, 'Theo's dead.'

She spun round. They faced each other, he gauging

her reaction, she assessing and accepting the truth in his
steady gaze before he enlarged, 'Three years ago this
summer—in a helicopter crash.'

There was no attempt to break it gently, no
compassion in his tone for her possible shock. Alex
reeled away again, this time towards the large windows
running along the side of the penthouse. Staring out
over the city, she concentrated on an uninspiring view
of other tall modern buildings. And the tears collected
for a flood in the back of her throat—for Theo, in an
upsurge of fond memories no longer blanketed by
bitterness; for Chris who had been right to keep faith—
three years, the man had said.

But she couldn't allow herself the luxury of shedding
them. Not yet. She could hear a glass tinkling behind
her, and the man softly treading towards her.

'Here, drink this.'

She accepted the brandy quickly, but he remained at
her shoulder, and when she raised her head, she
discovered his face reflected in the window pane. In the
glass his expression was softer . . . an illusion?

Dipping her eyes back to the brandy, she shut them
tight against the tears and took a deep reviving gulp
before moving to sit on an armchair. Her legs were
shaky but the possibility of showing vulnerability was
receding. She mustn't cry.

Kontos followed her over. 'I'm sorry, Miss Saunders,
I told you badly, but I didn't think . . .' he broke off his
stiff speech. It had been sincere enough, but he had
little talent for apologising and he was receiving no
encouragement from her bent head, seemingly preoccupied with warming the brandy in her glass.

'I'd give a damn,' she finished for him, and added
quickly, 'I'm fine.'

She almost sounded it. Evidently he believed so too,
or at least he ceased hovering over her to take the other
armchair that put the length of the coffee table between
them.

He lit a slim cigar and appraised her through a thin

veil of smoke before acknowledging coldly, 'You're very self-contained.'

Hard as nails he meant, and hard as nails he'd get, Alex resolved.

Raking into her bag, she began with, 'I presume Theo didn't rise from the grave to write this,' and tossed the letter she had received on the table.

Obviously its author, Kontos made no move to pick it up and replied to her underlying accusation with a smooth justification of, 'I wanted to ensure you would come.'

'Why now?' she retorted, thinking of what her sister had gone through, not knowing what had happened to Theo. 'You didn't bother with our other letters.'

'Sent three years ago?' he enquired, and when she confirmed it, went on to surmise, 'My mother would have dealt with those. I believe she may have destroyed Theo's mail unopened after the accident, especially if it came from England.'

Alex frowned with distrust. 'Why should she do that?'

'Something, or somebody, was obviously keeping Theo so long in England, and she resented the fact. More so after the crash deprived her of the chance of making up for his years of absence. I am certain, however, she had no knowledge of the child,' Kontos defended his mother's far-reaching action from the bitterness in Alex's expression. 'I myself did not know of your existence until the letter from your . . . friend aroused my interest. I suspected you might be in the same position with respect to myself, which is why I arranged a public meeting initially.'

Alex wished she still was. By 'friend' she assumed he must be referring to Chris. She wondered just how much he knew now.

'Can I see it?' she asked cagily. 'Chris's letter.'

He drew it from his inside pocket and handed it to her with a faintly sardonic lift to his eyebrows that could have implied anything.

Alex expected a love letter from a distracted, dying Chris but read:

'It's been a long time, Theo, too long to believe you will ever be coming back to England and too late to ask why. I am ill, dying perhaps. But Alex and Nicky, they will need your help. I send you his picture in the hope that you recall the first day you held your son and wept with the joy of him—surely that was real, if your love for his mother was not? That at least I must believe.

While I write this Alex is sitting with her head turned to the window to hide the cynicism in her eyes. If I could have hated you for anything, it would have been for putting it there. How short her share of happiness with us was, and how much she's had to pay for the few good times we gave her.

I beg you, Theo, take Nicky and give Alex a chance to be young and free again. She's done enough.
Chris.'

No dear Theo, no love Chris. Yet in a way it was a love letter—not directed at her husband or even her child. In the end it had been an older love that had counted the most—for her little sister Alex.

'Can I keep it?' Now there was a tremble in her voice, slight but discernible, because the letter brought back her loneliness for Chris.

Andros shrugged assent. 'This Chris—he is now dead?' he asked quietly.

Alex lifted vague eyes towards him. Chris? He? her mind echoed. But if he thought Chris male, then who was supposed to be Nicky's mother? It came to her slowly as she scanned the page again and saw how it could read to a stranger.

'Yes,' she nodded, and then hedged, 'How much do you know?'

His eyes narrowed on her. He had judged her upset by the letter of her 'friend', but the hard edge to her voice had returned.

'How much should I know?' he matched her curt tone.

'Nothing, as far as I'm concerned,' Alex replied obstructively.

'Good, by all means let us keep things simple.' He might be agreeing with her, but his irritation was plain in the tight line formed by his mouth. He came to the point with an abrupt, 'I want the boy.'

'What for?'

'What for!' he repeated angrily. 'He *is* my brother's son, is he not?' he demanded, and when Alex in turn didn't consider his enquiry worthy of a reply, continued harshly, 'Unless this Chris bears a remarkable resemblance to Theo?'

She followed him. What a nasty mind he had! Glaring, she began to set him straight. 'If you must know, Chris is . . . was my . . .'

'Your private life is your own business,' he cut in abrasively. 'Is the child Theo's or not? That's all I wish to be told.'

In the face of his overbearing arrogance, she stammered, 'But Chris wasn't . . .'

'I think, Miss Saunders, I should tell you what I do know before you are tempted to lie.' Again Alex opened her mouth to say something, but he swept on, 'After his first few months in London, Theo told the London hotel where he was training that he was moving from staff quarters to share a flat with a young man from his college course. Realising the information would be relayed to our father, he omitted to mention the other corner of the—shall we say—triangle.'

She sat in stunned silence for a minute, her brain repeating his words until an understanding dawned of the construction he had put on precious few facts and Theo's blatant lie. Why should Theo not have told his family about Chris?

Unintentionally damning herself further, she asked him, 'Was Theo married—before he came to England?'

'No,' he said, a sneer curving his lips. 'Didn't it occur
to you to ask *him* that, Miss Saunders?'

Ignoring his sarcasm, Alex spoke her thoughts aloud.
'Theo must have been too scared to tell his family the
truth.'

'He was sent to England to learn the hotel business,
not to ...' He halted in mid-speech, an exercise of
restraint as Alex obviously hit a sore point.

But she snapped it with her insolent prompting, 'Not
to what? Do tell!'

'Play around with some English girl either too stupid
or perhaps too cunning to take precautions,' he ground
out, no longer able to take a conciliating line with the
impossible girl. 'Satisfied?'

Alex, who had never slept with a man in her life,
took it with barely a flinch. He was so off target it was
almost amusing. Impassive, she stared at him.

'Are you waiting for an apology?' he rasped at her
continued silence.

'Why, are you going to give one?' she retorted coolly.

'No,' he barked back, pushing out of his chair. 'Is the
boy Theo's or not?'

'Yes,' she admitted shortly, tilting her head back
while he stood over her, leashed anger in every line of
his tall frame, 'but don't imagine I'm just going to hand
him over to you.'

'Hardly,' he conceded, and lost her in the process.
'How much?'

'How much?' she repeated, dazed.

'No more playing,' he harshly discounted her
confusion. 'A straight offer—ten thousand in cash and
the same every year you stay away from the boy.'

His words sunk in, slow and sure like a creeping
poison. Not only was the man prepared to buy his
nephew, he had actually conceived the absurd idea that
she was here to barter with him. What sort of person
would think like that?

'Dollars, drachmas or pounds?' she bit back, but
when it looked as though he was in danger of answering

her sarcasm in a serious vein, she rushed on, 'No, don't bother. I wouldn't sell you—*especially* you—a dog for that!'

Then she swept to the lift and hammered on the call button. Andros made no move to stop her. He didn't need to. When she at last forced herself to face him again, he stated the obvious. 'I locked it.'

'Then open it,' she ordered recklessly. 'I want to go back to my room,' and rid herself of the sight of him before she exploded!

'Almost convincing,' he drawled.

'What?'

'Never mind,' he dismissed, another insinuation left dangling. Alex had learned better than to beg enlightenment. He was appraising her flushed angry face and she assumed his hesitation was tactical, for there was no room for doubts in his firm, 'All right, fifteen thousand, and in sterling, of course; but that's the limit.'

He couldn't be serious! 'And if I refuse?'

'I *take* the boy from you,' he replied. No hesitation this time in the statement of intent.

He was serious but crazy too, Alex decided, scorning, 'You couldn't.'

'As I said before, try me,' he murmured, understated threat in the quiet words. 'I would sooner trade than go to court, but I shall if necessary, and with your past I shall win.'

She had him, smug arrogant brute that he was. 'And if my past was solely a figment of your warped imagination?'

He laughed unpleasantly. 'Academic, surely. Your only strength was being the boy's mother, but your placing the boy in an orphanage rendered it negligible.'

For the first time he hurt—bitterly. 'How do you know that?' And nothing else, Alex wondered.

'A friend in London checked that you and the boy were at the address in your friend's letter. Then when you didn't respond immediately to mine, I had him visit you,' he explained. 'You were out, but a neighbour told him the boy had been placed in a welfare institution. After that, I would have come to England and dealt with them directly, but apparently you had a change of . . . heart,' he finished on a derisive note.

'I . . . I couldn't manage,' she faltered.

'Frankly I don't want to hear excuses, and as a businessman I appreciate the profit motive, although in this case I scarcely applaud it.' He moved a little closer while Alex struggled for an articulate defence. In for the kill, she thought with the beginnings of rational fear of the man. He might be completely misinformed, but he was also so sure he was going to win; it was obviously his habit. He pressed on, 'I could instigate a full investigation if I wanted to know details, but I choose not to.'

He couldn't possibly be hoping for gratitude for that concession; instead she scowled, 'Why not?'

'Reasons you wouldn't understand,' he said disparagingly.

But he had underestimated Alex's intelligence—or perhaps intuition was nearer the mark as she retorted, anger for Chris uppermost, 'You want to pretend Nicky was a virgin birth, right?' She savoured his momentarily startled expression and saw the truth plain and damning in it before she finished, 'Only in this case your brother was the virgin!'

'You put things so well, *Miss* Saunders.'

Now she had it all. He despised her for living with Theo and the non-existent Chris, bearing Nicky outside marriage and then dumping him in an orphanage to be later retrieved for the most despicable of motives. She had the full picture of his thinking. And he had exactly nothing!

And if she told him the truth—that Nicky was not her son nor the bastard he presumed without question? Oh, it would make a difference—of course it would. She saw that quite clearly. It would make it that much easier for him to take Nicky away!

She wanted to tell him to go somewhere warm and damned, but she was too cautious to do that. Instead she stated baldly, 'Okay, I'll trade.'

It caught him off guard, although it was supposedly what he wanted to hear, and his black brows drew together. The man was suspicious of everything—or maybe she had capitulated a shade too abruptly.

'But not at that price.' She grew into the part, letting her eyes range about the luxury of her surroundings. 'You can afford more—twenty thousand, I'd say.'

And then brought them back to his, invested with all the bold insolence she could muster. She forced herself to stand her ground when she imagined she saw the desire to hit her returned even while he appeared to have what he wanted. His believing was all that counted. It would disarm him long enough for her to get away from Greece as easily as he had lured her there.

She had it. His mouth curved with mockery, or was it self-derision, when he admitted. 'For a couple of minutes, Miss Saunders, I wondered if I'd made a mistake about you.'

'You—make a mistake, Mr Kontos?' Alex replied archly, and before he could retaliate, pursued, 'We have a deal?'

'Yes.' He nodded and held back on saying anything that might jeopardise it, although he felt the girl laughing at him as clearly as if she had done it out loud. If it hadn't been for the circumstances, the boy, he would have accepted it as a challenge, a different scenario in mind for himself and this strangely attractive girl. Sanity prevailed as he announced, 'In the morning I shall call my lawyer and he will formalise the arrangement.'

'Fine,' Alex muttered with breezy unconcern for his plans. She wouldn't be around to play a part in them. 'Now can I go back to my room?'

He unlocked the lift and entered with her, forestalling her protest with, 'I'll escort you back.'

'There's no need,' Alex replied ungraciously.

'Probably not,' he agreed drily, as the lift doors closed on them, and pushed the down button.

There was an insult in his succinct comment if one cared to look for it, but Alex didn't. She was too tired, too frayed at the edges by the gruelling evening. They walked together through the public areas of the hotel, up in the guests' lift and along the corridor to her suite without exchanging a single word. Alex wondered if his nerves were also affected by the tension, heightened rather than diminished by the now total lack of communication between them.

She was just deciding this Kontos man didn't have nerves to be stretched when he ended the silence within a yard of her door.

'Can I come in and see the boy?'

'Why?' She spun round and read the answer in his expression, wide open to her as she turned so quickly—and wished she hadn't as she stopped believing him to be one hundred per cent cold arrogance. To her maybe he was, but what would he be to Nicky, his own flesh and blood?

Nothing, she vowed as she shut out that fleeting glimpse of humanity in his overly handsome face; her claim was stronger.

'He's sleeping,' she stated, defensive when she intended to be hard.

'I won't wake him,' he promised quietly. 'I just want to look at him again.'

To verify his likeness to Theo? flitted into Alex's mind. Yet he hadn't asked for any real proof of Nicky's parentage other than her word and his strong similarity to his brother. And suddenly she understood why; the man wanted Nicky to be his nephew just as much as she wished he wasn't. It made her lose taste for the whole rotten contest between them.

'He's a restless sleeper and he might get a scare if he wakes up suddenly,' she said more anxiously than obstinately, as her divine right to be the winner became blurred with conscience.

It was Andros Kontos who sharpened it with a sceptical, 'You care?'

'He's my flesh and blood too, you know,' she cried unthinkingly, passionately, forgetting she had just ostensibly sold her rights over Nicky. 'And you're six years late on the scene!'

He was staring down at her, puzzled rather than angry, although he clearly recognised the nature of her accusation because he responded, 'I'll make it up.'

'How? Expensive presents? Spoiling?' she scoffed rashly, slipping out of her supposed character and failing to quite make it back with. 'Still, that's your business.'

He snatched her arm before she could reach the door handle and turned her back towards him. He seemed to be searching her face. She didn't feel it gave anything more away as she set her mouth into sullenness, but he murmured all the same, 'Am I wrong?'

'About what?' she rapped back.

'About you.' He was looking at her so closely, feature by feature, that willpower alone made her stay still. And then he did something totally unreal, lifting a strand of her long fair hair and running its silky natural texture through his fingers, before observing in a soft undertone, 'You don't fit, Alex Saunders.'

Because her hair wasn't dyed? Or her face wasn't painted? Or simply because his gesture seemed disturbingly intimate and brought a deep involuntary blush to her pale cheeks? She jerked her hair from his light hold.

He still pursued, 'Why is that?'

It was another chance to tell him the truth, but it passed by as she lapsed back into flippancy. 'It's always difficult to live up to other people's stereotypes, especially when one is suffering from jet lag. Goodnight.'

And she left him alone to interpret it how he pleased, as she slipped quickly into the suite. She didn't want him to know her better, know her at all. She didn't want to know more about him either. Let them keep things simple, as he himself had suggested.

There could only be one winner—the more ruthless of the two—and she wasn't going to lose much-needed sleep over ensuring that it would be her.

CHAPTER THREE

WITH no more than half her normal quota of sleep Alex's weary body protested as she emerged from the fog of fitful wakening. She had left a wide gap between the bedroom curtains and her bleary eyes blinked against the sun already infiltrating the room in a direct line to her face.

Searching blind for her watch, she swung her bare feet on to the soft carpet and reassured herself that it was still early despite that brightness. Not yet six, in fact. For a blank moment between sleep and full waking she failed to pinpoint why she had to rise at this unearthly hour—and then the events of the previous evening came rushing back to motivate her tired legs in the direction of the bathroom.

She stayed long enough under the shower to wash away her drowsiness, before dressing quickly in white jeans and matching cotton shirt with a masculine cut. Its bagginess was cinched in at the waist with a wide cloth belt and she looped her damp hair back with a thin band of blue ribbon.

Just like every morning of her life, she wasted no time on what she would wear, but today she did something quite unusual for breezy self-confident Alex Saunders— she stared long and hard at herself in a mirror. Unconsciously at first, she posed, hands on hips, twisting this way and that in front of the bathroom mirror, and critically examined the figure in white. Slim and leggy but not too boyish with the vague outline of her breasts showing, and the face, fair-lashed and browed, eyes a vivid blue and the straight neat nose above a more generous mouth.

She didn't discover anything new about herself even after she acknowledged that was the purpose of the exercise. She could take herself apart, feature by feature, and then concentrate on the whole, and still not be able to type herself from her own criterion, or more to the point, anyone else's. She gave up trying when she admitted to herself through whose eyes she had been attempting to visualise herself. What did it matter what *he* thought, with his narrow prejudices?

She walked back through to the bedroom to wake Nicky. His head was buried face down in the pillow, and she gently shifted him on to his back, still asleep, his mouth moving very slightly as he dreamed. Good dreams? Bad dreams?—it was difficult to tell. He always looked so vulnerable in sleep.

As she watched those small movements of his lips, it started up again—that litany that had whispered through her mind in the sleepless hours after midnight. She had worked her college holidays, Saturdays when she could get a part-time job during term, to contribute more than her grant to the household budget; that counted. She had sat up nights through more than the usual childhood illnesses when Chris was working or not well enough to do it; that counted more. She loved Nicky completely, unreservedly, as her own; and that counted most.

So why did she even bother stacking what Andros Kontos and his wealth could offer against her love?

She pulled herself up from the edge of the bed and sorted through the suitcase for fresh shorts and tee-shirt, and again lost her decisiveness in the act of withdrawing them from the battered bag. Like her own clothing, much of the little boy's was rescued from market stalls and jumble sales. He never complained, although they seldom fitted him properly; he accepted it as normal—other people's clothes. For how long? Till he was nine, twelve, sixteen? Alex caught herself questioning, and immediately tried to stifle the doubts. Clothes didn't matter, and even if they did, long before then she would have their lives straightened out—a good job, a flat, money. She already had some, the bait money that had been far in excess of the economy tickets she had bought; she was certainly not going to be high-principled and stupid enough to hand it back. It would give them a start.

She slowly shook Nicky awake and more or less had to force him under the unfamiliar shower. When she was sure he was quite alert, she handed him soap and sponge, leaving the door ajar. By the time, however, she collected his clothes, he was giggling like a mad thing. It brought an indulgent smile to her lips—his first shower to be considered such a treat—but the pleasure faded as another doubt crept unsought, unwanted into her head. How many other firsts would have to wait till adulthood, perhaps wait for ever?

Allowing him ten minutes more to enjoy himself, she returned from packing to find him drinking the water straight into his uptilted mouth.

'Yuk! How can you?' she shuddered with disgust.

'It's cold,' he spluttered through a mouthful of water, and sure enough when Alex tested the water it was icy. In her absence the temperature dial had been experimented with.

She hauled him quickly out of the shower and rubbed him briskly, ignoring his grumbles at her roughness.

'It was funny, Lex, like pins and needles,' he volunteered for her education. 'Funny, but sort of nice.'

'Masochist,' she muttered to herself.

'What's a mas'chist?' Nicky picked up inaccurately.

Twenty impossible questions before breakfast was Nicky's norm. One down and nineteen to go, Alex groaned inwardly, but she returned with a mischief and an honesty he couldn't possibly understand, 'Someone who likes to get their bottom slapped,' and aimed a playful tap on his behind that had him protesting loudly, 'No, I don't, Lex! No, I don't!' but giggling all the same. His aunt Alex had a way of teasing that was fun even when it didn't make sense.

She gave a last rough towel to his damp curls and checked that the rest of him was warm and dry as a bone. After a winter of chest complaints, she wasn't taking any risks.

'Come on, Nick, get dressed,' she ordered more sharply than usual.

'You angry, Lex?' he asked then, mouth down at the corners.

She pulled the tee-shirt over his head. 'No, just don't do anything so silly again. O.K.?'

'Because of my cough?' It was mildly challenging, but when she failed to say anything one way or the other, there was a definite sullenness in his, 'I haven't had one for ages and ages . . . years!'

Two months, Alex could have reminded but didn't. He hated being ill and treated as fragile. And this morning she didn't want to scold him.

In the end she didn't have to search for an opener to tell Nicky they were leaving and why. When she was busy gathering up toothbrushes, soap and sponge, he had wandered back into the bedroom and was staring at the suitcase on the bed, open but neatly packed ready for their departure.

'Is my daddy coming to take me to the island, Lex?' His eyes moved from the bag to her.

No nice way; she told him straight. 'I'm sorry, Nick, I didn't know—Daddy's not . . . Daddy's dead.'

She didn't have to expand on it, go into the whys and wherefores. The information was received with stony silence and a flicker of resignation, as though it was no more or less than he might have expected.

And then she was kneeling on the carpet before him and he was flinging himself at her, bony arms reaching round her neck in a frantic hug.

'Don't leave me, Lex,' was sobbed against her throat. 'Please don't leave me! Love *you* best of all.'

'I won't, pet,' she choked out, returning his hug nearly as hard as he was giving it.

'Never!' he urged fiercely. 'Say never, Lex!'

'Never, ever, ever . . .' she repeated over and over, and it wasn't just comforting for the child. She loved him. She needed him too. And if it was selfish, what she was doing, she couldn't help herself.

Alex knew enough about hotels to reckon on there being a skeleton staff round the reception desk at quarter to seven in the morning. She wavered between walking out under their noses, suitcases in hand, to hope for a taxi in the street, or going boldly up to the desk and asking them to call one. She decided on the latter, assuming quite rightly that Andros Kontos would not be haunting the lobby at this hour. Owner, not manager, he had called himself.

Nevertheless she took a minor precaution.

'So you've got that, Nicky? Down to the ground floor, walk to the door and wait for me at the bottom of the steps.'

'Why, Lex?' the boy asked, looking up and down the deserted corridor of the first floor with a quick nervous glance. He had caught some of Alex's mood; they were playing spies or something.

'Just do it, Nick, right?' she pressed.

'Right,' he agreed, a smile emerging, and went on in an excited whisper, 'Are they after us?'

'Who?' Alex looked blank for a second and then wished she hadn't started all this cloak and dagger stuff, even if it had cheered Nicky up. Was it necessary? Kontos couldn't really prevent them from leaving, could he?

'Yes, it's a game, Nick,' she improvised hurriedly, 'And if one of them stops you in the lobby, you say your mother is waiting outside, and if anyone asks why you're hanging round the steps, I'm inside and you're waiting for me. Understand?'

'Sort of.' He screwed up his face in concentration. It seemed a dumb kind of game to him, but if Alex wanted to play it, that was good enough reason. He repeated her instructions, or at last an abridged version. 'If I'm inside, you're outside. And if I'm outside, you're inside. Right, Lex?'

'Something like that,' she returned his grin. 'Now off you go—and remember, don't move from the hotel entrance.'

She held the lift door for him, pressed the button for the ground floor and quickly withdrew her hand. Waiting for the lift to come up again, she felt more confident. Even if Andros had instructed his staff to keep tabs on their movements, surely she would be anonymous to the early shift of workers, without Nicky in tow.

At her first hurdle, however, she had reason to wonder, and almost bolted before the clerk could excuse his staring, 'Madam is up early.'

Deciphering his Greek, Alex breathed a sigh of relief. She'd never seen him before; he was simply surprised at her early rising.

'Yes—yes, I am,' she dredged up some Greek and sent him a winning smile. 'It's a lovely day.'

Eyes on her fair skin and hair, he switched to a hesitant English. 'Madam wants breakfast? We shall open the dining room.'

Madam was starving, but breakfast would have to wait. With reckless abandon and a smoothness she herself applauded, Alex told him lie after lie: Madam didn't have time for breakfast; she had a flight to catch to Rome, could he call a taxi; she had already taken care of her bill last night. *He* seemed to swallow it whole, but still Alex's luck had run out.

Stavros was half asleep but for a grumbling self-conscious that was calling him a fool for swapping his shift with another porter. Sullenly he listened to the desk clerk rapping out an order to check if there was a taxi available for the lady. For one second—it couldn't have been more—his eyes passed over the girl. But that was all it needed, for Stavros had an eye for a pretty woman.

It *was* the same one, he told himself as he walked towards the lift doors. But where was the boy, if it was? He had the answer as he exited the hotel. He hesitated on the top step.

No one knew the *patron*'s interest in the English girl; no one would have dared ask. But there had been gossip, especially with the boy as dark as any Greek. And if he wanted to know when the woman arrived, wouldn't he be just as interested in her leaving? Perhaps he already knew; perhaps not. It was very early. Maybe Stavros could do himself some good; or maybe he could get himself fired. He tossed a mental coin, and it came down heads. Alex lost.

The desk clerk shot him a look of personal recrimination for reporting, falsely, the street empty of taxis and while he called the local taxi service that assured him that two of their cars had already been despatched to the hotel, and the girl worriedly checked her watch, Stavros took an enormous risk. It paid off.

Some quarter of an hour later Alex had checked her watch a dozen times when Stavros announced that her taxi had arrived. He picked up her suitcase and went into his set piece just as they reached the steps.

'Your little boy, he wanted to sit in taxi, madam,' he said at the exact moment Alex's eyes anxiously swept the empty pavement.

Due to a sudden unusual demand for taxis, or at least for them to circle the block passengerless for a short while, there was only one car in the immediate vicinity, and Alex was too impatient to be gone to challenge its validity.

It was large and dark blue, with smoked windows that kept the sun out on the inside. And naturally prying eyes from the outside.

For a couple of seconds she froze, half in and half out of the car, and rejected what she saw. Could she have been that naïve, that easy to trap?

The man in the back seat spoke first. 'Your choice, Miss Saunders. Get in quietly and close the door, or we shall drive off without you.'

Andros Kontos's voice broke through her numb shock, but she didn't obey even when she heard the car's engine firing, the driver having left her door to quickly stow away her case and then install himself behind the wheel. He just couldn't do this, could he?

'Let him go!' she hissed angrily while Nicky wriggled more desperately to free himself from his captor, and then with genuine horror, she shrieked, 'For God's sake, you barbarian, take your hand off his mouth!'

Perhaps some urgency in her cry got through, for he allowed the little boy to start screaming, 'Lex! Lex!' at the top of his lungs, but he kept his arm circled round Nicky's chest.

'Make up your mind,' he growled, low and harsh, but discernible beneath Nicky's childish pitch.

She didn't have to; Nicky's rasped breaths between screams made it for her, and there was no way in this world she could have known that Andros Kontos himself was on the verge of capitulation.

He slipped his hold the moment she closed the door, and watched as the boy scrambled as far from him as he could on to Alex's knee.

'You bastard!' she mouthed as the car accelerated away, and then ignored him totally.

Cradling the boy with one arm, she murmured repetitively, 'It's all right, Nick, it's all right,' while her free hand searched her handbag. The boy's screaming stopped, but the laboured breathing didn't. She spilled her handbag's contents on the space between Kontos and herself, and at last found the inhaler. Stroking the boy's hair, she implored, 'Calm down, Nick, and suck ... harder ... that's it.'

Soothing and encouraging the child, she felt the man watching them, his guilt almost tangible in the air, till Nicky's struggle for breath quietened to a gentle sucking of the plastic inhaler she had put in his mouth. She confined herself to a brief shake of her head when the Greek asked if a doctor was needed, and a shrug when he enquired if the attack was psychosomatic.

In all probability, Alex thought, it had been caused by the fright he had given Nicky; but it could, just maybe, have been the delayed physical shock of his earlier cold shower. Whichever, she couldn't trust herself yet to speak without shouting, and that could start Nicky off again.

Bracing him more comfortably against her arm, she asked, 'Better, Nick?' and removed the inhaler at his nod.

'Is he one of them?' was the first thing he said, in one of his loud whispers.

'No, Nicky,' she dismissed quickly.

'I told him you were inside like you said, but *he* said you wanted me to wait in the car,' Nicky went into his explanation, worried he'd got it wrong somewhere. 'And then when I tried to call out to you, he put his hand over my mouth. And I got scared because I thought he must be one of them.'

Andros Kontos made no attempt to enter the conversation, but Alex did not miss his quizzical frown.

'No, he's not,' she repeated more firmly, anxious to get off that subject before Nicky started going into detail.

Now her simple plan seemed simple in the worst sense of the word. She summed up their present predicament and made the best of it by forcing out, 'He's a friend of ours.'

Nicky thought about it for a moment and came back with, 'Why did he put his hand over my mouth, then?'

Alex switched her eyes from the top of Nicky's head to Andros Kontos, challenging him to play a part in some charade for the boy's benefit. Nicky imitated her action, swivelling in her lap to stare straight at the man, in the same 'well, we're waiting' attitude.

The man's response was directed at Nicky. 'I apologise for the crassness of my behaviour. It was more reflex than intentional.'

Said in precise, well-spoken English, but it might as well have been Greek to Nicky. He turned to Alex for a translation and she offered, 'He means he's sorry, and he won't do it again.'

'Oh,' a less than convinced mumble from Nicky, but Andros flashed her a look remarkably like gratitude.

He could keep it! Alex's eyes did not grow one degree warmer as she stared back at him.

'How often does he get these attacks?' he queried with a deep frown.

'Now and again.' Not a very comprehensive reply, but Alex did not feel very forthcoming.

His gaze fell away from Alex to examine his nephew's pale thin face before he pursued, 'He is prone to illness?'

'I don't get ill,' Nicky declared.

Aggressive as well as loud, the interruption was met with raised disapproving eyebrows from the man who clearly thought well-brought-up children only spoke when spoken to.

'He looks sickly to me,' he said over his nephew's head.

Alex hastened to get in first with a wry, 'But he isn't deaf.'

'Meaning?' the man clipped out.

'Oh, nothing!' she snapped when her heavy hint went astray.

'Nothing,' Nicky echoed with an unusual impudence. He wasn't scared of the man now Alex was there and he had decided for himself that the man wasn't *his* friend. But when his aunt abruptly told him to shut up, he mumbled, 'Yes, Lex,' and did so.

Andros, however, muttered critically, 'The boy lacks manners.'

And had Alex wondering if he was going out of his way to alienate his nephew as quickly as he possibly could. So why stop him? she thought nastily.

No logical reason, but she did. 'I don't think a crash course right this second would be a good idea, do you?' she enquired with an acid sweetness. There, if he didn't take her advice she wasn't going to give any more.

His eyes narrowed on her, evidently disliking her tone, but he managed a bare sort of civility to agree, 'Perhaps you are right, Miss Saunders.'

Alex could have felt a malicious satisfaction but

strangely didn't. Analysed, her prime emotion was
absurd—why on earth feel sorry for Andros Kontos
because he hadn't the first clue about children? The
absurdity, however, fitted well with the day so far, so
she excused it.

She bent her head to whisper in Nicky's ear and when
he nodded with heavy reluctance, she said aloud, 'Do
you think you could tell your driver to stop so Nicky
can ride in the front for a while?'

'Why?' was the abrupt response.

Alex bypassed several sarcastic replies as she read
the suspicion in his expression, to mutter tautly, 'He
wants to,' and shot Nicky a glance that dared him to
deny it.

With another sceptical look at both of them Andros
slid the glass partition between the two halves of the car
and addressed his driver in rapid Greek. The exchange
was effected briskly, with Kontos taking the boy out on
his side of the lay-by and ordering Alex to stay where
she was.

She obeyed in stony silence, but the second he slid the
partition shut on Nicky and the driver, she bit out
angrily, 'I wouldn't be so idiotic!'

'Really?' he challenged.

'You have our case in the boot,' she enlarged with an
insultingly slow drawl. 'We appear to be somewhere on
the outskirts of Athens, and I've forgotten my A to Z.
Where in heaven's name would we run to?'

'I apologise,' he eventually said with a stunning
mildness.

'What?' It was incredulous.

'Surely you don't need a translation too, Miss
Saunders,' he continued with an urbanity that had Alex
gritting her teeth. 'I am sorry that I believed you were
considering a dramatic bid for freedom. In the
circumstances, you have behaved most reasonably.'

'I . . .' she faltered, disconcerted.

'And for what it's worth, I also regret hurting my . . .
your son,' he conceded stiffly; but before she could

decide whether he meant it, he added, 'You didn't tell him anything about me, did you?'

Now *that* she could rail against. 'What did you expect? To give him a choice between a rich uncle or myself? For pity's sake, he's only six years old, in case you hadn't noticed!'

'Meaning?' he demanded.

She snapped back, 'Would you stop saying that? It's getting on my nerves.'

He turned icy eyes in her direction. 'Saying what?'

'Oh, never mind,' she dismissed shortly, and began to rescue her clutter from the back seat and the floor where it had rolled, only to have her hand clutched by hard strong fingers.

When she jerked her head up, he rasped, 'No woman ... no person has ever spoken to me like that before, Alex Saunders!' His fingers tightened painfully. 'I do not think I like it.'

'Are you threatening me?' she gasped. She tugged on her hand and he hurt her some more.

'Do you feel threatened?' he said with a voice like silk.

For seconds, yes, she did—lost courage so radically she felt the arm he was holding tremble under his strength. And he felt it too.

It was enough for him now. Satisfied, he slowly unfurled his fingers so Alex could slip his grip.

He said what he was thinking. 'For the moment, I shall make allowances for your nationality.'

'Thank you,' Alex muttered, leaving him to decide if she was being sarcastic or not, and stared stupidly when he did another reversal and began to help her pick up her scattered possessions. He caught her expression and handing over her comb and Chris's letter, he commented with some of her own dryness, 'I do not lack manners,' and when she murmured a grudging thanks, added, 'Nor, you will find, am I a total barbarian.'

Alex blushed involuntarily. She supposed that must

have been one of the insults she had hurled at him. Was
he keeping a mental stock of them? If so, he'd better
have a good memory.

'What are you doing?' she exclaimed, although she
could see full well what he was doing—rifling the purse
wallet he had retrieved from the floor.

'How much is mine?' he asked coolly, extracting the
paper money from its pocket, and in front of a stunned
Alex, counting the notes and traveller's cheques. 'All of
it, I should imagine. Yes?'

Every penny, and she wasn't about to beg him to put
it back. 'You're going to take it anyway, aren't you?'
she replied sourly.

'Unless you intend sticking to the deal I was under
the impression we made last night?' he queried in the
same even tone.

'Go to . . .' she broke off as her arm was once more
taken in his bruising grip to silence her.

'My allowances do not stretch to swearing,' he
informed her.

'You're hurting me,' she muttered through clenched
teeth.

'That is the general idea,' he claimed, so calm she saw
he was punishing her without any real anger. 'Has no
one ever told you, Alex Saunders, that you must bend
before you break? No more swearing, agreed?'

Silent cursing didn't count, Alex decided as she was
forced to nod her head for the release of her arm.
Damned arrogant sadistic brute!

'You wish to know where we are going?' he said after
Alex had fallen into a resentful silence.

'Does it matter?' she muttered offhandedly.

'I would have thought so.' He gave her a searching
glance.

She looked away but matched his quiet tone. 'I could
point out that you're committing a crime by abducting
us, but I'm sure you're aware of it. I could demand that
you turn the car round and take us to the airport, but
something tells me I'd be wasting my breath. So no, I

don't really think it matters where in particular you're taking us.'

'You have a point,' he responded in near amused tones. 'Perhaps it is time I credited you with some intelligence.'

'As you like,' Alex replied icily. She wasn't about to credit *him* with anything!

'And remember you are unpredictable,' he said as though he was weighing her up as an opponent. He probably was.

'Not unpredictable enough, it seems,' she answered with a touch of bitterness.

Andros read her thoughts with an ease that was a little disturbing and surprised her by admitting, 'Oh, I might have suspected there was something wrong last night, but you were a jump ahead of me this morning. If it hadn't been for one of my staff recognising you . . .'

'You weren't waiting for me?'

He ran a hand over the dark stubble on his cheekbone. 'Do I look as though I was ready for you?'

As well as unshaven, Alex noticed he was tieless. Indeed his white shirt was deeply slashed to show more dark hair curled tightly against his chest.

She didn't realise she had stared a little too long at his dishevelled appearance until he murmured, 'I hope my state of undress does not offend you, Miss Saunders.'

Quickly averting her eyes, she retorted, 'Hardly, you know me,' and thought, let him make what he liked out of it.

'Do I?' he challenged drily. 'Presuming you have recovered from your—what was it now?—ah, yes, jet lag,' his eyes ran over her fair natural looks, 'you are still failing to live up to your stereotype.'

'Disappointed?' she sneered, not pleased to have her taunts used against her.

'I don't know yet,' he was slow in replying, taking her sarcasm literally, and throwing her further off balance with, 'I haven't decided whether you amuse or irritate me, Miss Saunders.'

If his current tone was anything to go by she was amusing the hell out of him, and she disliked him even more for it. She saw nothing remotely funny about the situation.

'So what are your plans?' she demanded.

'Plans?' he echoed, bland in the face of her sharpness.

Alex felt her temper slipping again as she returned caustically, 'I presume you are going to stop short of murdering me to ensure custody of Nicky.'

'Possibly,' was the slow deliberate reply, and when Alex reacted for a second with complete credulity, blue eyes widening with alarm, he gave her an equally slow deliberate smile.

Definitely amusing him, damn him! she swore silently as she tried to quieten her heart to its normal beat. Not that she had really believed his mockery, she assured herself, but the man was outside her experience—as unpredictable to her as she was apparently to him.

'My plans are flexible,' he murmured at last.

'What exactly does that mean?' she scowled.

'It means, Miss Saunders,' he drawled on what could only be described as a note of boredom, 'It is . . .' he checked the gold watch on his wrist, '. . . slightly before eight o'clock in the morning, I have yet to have my breakfast owing to your impetuous behaviour, and I never make decisions on an empty stomach.'

Banal or absurd, it was a conversation stopper.

CHAPTER FOUR

THEY had left Athens miles behind, thirty or forty—
Alex wasn't sure. The car was climbing up a hillside as
the road, little more than a dirt track now, followed a
natural crevice in the ancient rock of southern Greece—
higher and higher until they approached the headland.

And there below, so far below as they rounded the
crest, was the Mediterranean, a clear blue shimmering
in the heat. From their height, the view was spectacular,
an assault on the senses, with a whisper of a
breeze touching her face and smelling of sea, salty and
clean.

For a moment in its enjoyment she forgot everything
else—and then Andros's voice drifted into her
absorption,

'Beautiful, no?'

She turned her head to catch him watching her,
apparently as absorbed as she had been in the scenery.
Immediately her eyes grew cold and hostile, and she left
his question to hang, wondering what had been in her
expression to make him ask it.

Beautiful, yes, she silently acknowledged as she
returned to staring fixedly out of the side window. But
where were they?

Around the next bend, the car left the twisting road
and joined another, sloping gently downwards, narrower
but tarred all the same. There had been no signpost,
and the incongruity of the modern road in the primitive
countryside surrounding did nothing to placate a rising
sense of panic. Perhaps it was sensible to feel it, that
fine thread of fear running up her spine—to stop telling
herself he couldn't possibly kidnap them in broad
daylight and start accepting that he had. And do
what?—wait, she supposed, for she could hardly

begin planning an escape from a prison she had yet to see.

That particular situation was remedied as she glimpsed the brick-red tiled roof of a building, appearing and disappearing through the engulfing greenery of semi-tropical plants permitted to grow wild to shield its privacy. The road ended abruptly at a squat stone garage, and still the house remained partially secluded, as it was on a level below, bound by a high perimeter fence.

There was little else she could do but climb out of the car as instructed and she found herself before a gate in the fence, already unlocked and swung wide by Andros's driver. Poised at the top of the flight of steps leading to the two-storied villa built on a plateau in the hillside, Alex swerved her head round and then back, realising it could not be seen from the public road above but only from the seashore far beneath them. Sensible or not, her mind was for seconds gripped by her imagination running wild, and her body felt the impulse to do the same, only when she backed from the steps, it was to be steadied by a firm hand at her elbow.

'It's all right,' he reassured her.

'All right' was scarcely how she would have described her predicament, Alex thought, anger displacing fear in part, as they descended the stairway, and she wondered what exactly he had meant by a remark she considered almost inane. Nothing was all right!

Halfway down there was a landing that met with the wide balcony surrounding the upper storey of the villa, and he steered them round to the front of the building.

'The sea, Lex!' Nicky exclaimed in awed tones.

'Yes,' Alex murmured, sharing some of his breathlessness, for if the view from the car had been spectacular, the range from their current vantage-point was out of this world. Or out of her world, at any rate, she realised, assimilating miles of blue sea stretching

endlessly in the distance and struggling to overcome
what could only be termed culture shock.

She had lived all her life within the sights and sounds
of one of the busiest cities in Europe, now she was
standing on the balcony of a villa built into a hillside in
the middle of nowhere, and nothing had prepared her
for its magnificent isolation.

Andros went the length of the balcony, unlocking
and folding back the wooden shutters, one by one
sliding back the contrastingly modern patio doors to
expose the house to light and air, and then he came
back to where they were standing. Alex sensed him
watching her again, perhaps for her reaction, and she
hoped she didn't look as awed as Nicky evidently was.

She felt the silence between them uncomfortable
enough to ask, 'Who lives here normally?'

Andros surprised her with his, 'I do,' and noted it by
adding with a trace of mocking amusement, 'Why?
Who did you expect?'

'Nobody,' she shrugged, a sullen set to her mouth as
she prayed he could not guess at some of her more
dramatic imaginings 'It's very different from the
penthouse,' she commented defensively.

'And you think it more my style?' he queried.

'Perhaps.'

'And how would you describe it?' he encouraged,
eyes speculative.

She was tempted, sorely, as an image of the
penthouse came to mind, even when she understood he
was asking for more than her opinion of four walls and
some luxurious pieces of furniture. She knew how
provocative words like sterile and characterless would
be, but restrained her reply to, 'I don't think you'd
make allowances if I told you what I think.'

If he recognised it as insolence he chose to treat it
with a bland approving, 'Good. You're learning
already,' and it was all Alex could do to stop herself
unlearning and taking an angry swipe at his arrogant
face. She must have betrayed it, for his eyes slid from

hers to the hands clenched at her side and then back again before he dropped his amused tone to state, 'I think, however, it is going to be a slow process.'

How slow Alex showed him by retorting, 'Why, do you think *I* lack manners as well?'

For a second it was debatable who was more liable to hit the other, but Nicky, silent forgotten observer of the exchange, chose that moment to tug at her trouser leg and announce shyly, 'I need the toilet, Lex.'

It snapped the tension between them, but Andros Kontos's contemptuous gaze lingered on Alex just long enough to convey exactly how lacking he regarded her, before he grabbed Nicky's hand and whipped him through the nearest room.

He moved so quickly it had her wondering if he thought Nicky wasn't house-trained either, and she was seething at the idea as she caught him up outside the bathroom in which he had installed Nicky. When he instructed her to follow him as he threw wide each bedroom door off the inside corridor, she dragged her feet with a show of heavy reluctance.

'Take your pick,' he ordered brusquely. 'You may be here for a while.'

'I don't think so.'

'We will see,' he said evenly, but his narrowed eyes seemed to note the challenge in her tone. Then he curled a hand round her arm to guide her to the bedroom off the centre of the balcony. 'This one gets the most light and has the best view of the sea.'

Both statements were true, and the room itself was more than pleasant, with its cool whitewashed walls and parquet floor scattered with Indian weave rugs. The bed was wide and low, covered with a cream spread, and the furniture of natural wood. Its very simplicity appealed to Alex, but she said nothing until Andros prompted impatiently, 'You like it?'

And then it was to mutter, 'Ever the gracious hotelier, only it sticks in my throat to play one of your satisfied guests.'

She did not, however, expect him to close the gap between them, and hold her arms just tight enough to stop her pulling away.

His voice was casual as he stared down at her defiant face and murmured, 'Tell me this, Alex Saunders, have you ever been struck by a man?'

At first she simply widened her eyes in shock at the question, delivered with a cool mockery that somehow made it more intimidating than if he had been blazingly angry. There was a shameful waver in her eventual denial of, 'No, of course not,' and when he lifted his hand, she acted reflexively.

It never came, the blow from which she'd flinched, and she was left feeling foolish—like a skittish fear-filled animal, as the back of his fingers trailed lightly down her cheek and he remarked with dry amusement, 'Now that does surprise me,' before putting her almost gently away from him.

It was similar to the trick he had played on her earlier, making her afraid of him, only to laugh when she betrayed her fears so that they appeared the product of an over-active imagination. But this time she understood that behind the unpleasantness of his humour there was an even more unpleasant warning. She was being told she could push so far, and no farther.

Yet when Nicky reappeared at the balcony window he surprised her by saying, 'I'll leave you to explain the situation to the boy before we have breakfast.'

'You trust me?'

A short derisive laugh dismissed the idea out of hand. 'No, but there's little I can do to prevent your giving him any version of the truth you choose.'

What a low opinion of her he had, Alex fumed as he strode out of the room. So why shouldn't she live up to it? They had been kidnapped and were his prisoners, no matter if the villa was a far cry from a more traditional gaol.

How far she was to appreciate fully when Nicky,

taking her hand, urged, 'Wait till you see it, Lex!' and dragged her out along the balcony to see the 'it' he had already discovered.

'It's a swimming pool,' the boy explained unnecessarily as they stood side by side at the balcony railing; below them was a pool of clear blue water.

Alex laughed her surprise. 'It certainly is!'

'How do they get the water into it?' Nicky asked in the same amazed tone.

'I don't know, kiddo,' Alex shook her head. She could just about envisage how the house built into the cliff face could have been constructed with the help of cranes, but the technicalities of providing fresh water for the luxury of a swimming pool in this lonely primitive spot completely defeated her.

'Are we staying here, Lex?' Nicky pursued, not sounding too grieved at the prospect.

'Yes, for a while, perhaps,' she was purposely vague.

'With the man?' She nodded and wasn't overly surprised when his face fell and he announced quite positively, 'I don't like him.'

Her conscience didn't extend to extolling Andros Kontos's virtues—even if she had noticed any—but Alex did chide mildly, 'You don't know him yet, Nick.'

His reply startled her. 'He doesn't like you, Lex.'

Out of the mouths of babes, Alex groaned, but she was quick to force a soft laugh. 'What gave you that idea, love?'

'He looks at you funny,' Nicky declared.

Alex had no difficulty interpreting that particular 'funny' as 'funny nasty' and couldn't contradict Nicky's observation outright. But at all costs she wanted to keep the child out of any wrangling.

'You know how I get mad with you when you're bad?' she started tentatively, and when he smiled sheepishly, she continued, 'But I still like you afterwards, don't I? Well, sometimes I make that man angry in the same way, but it doesn't mean he doesn't like me.'

'Like when you hit him in the park?' Nicky volunteered, and at her hesitation, added, 'He was really mad then, remember?'

Of course she did. She could scarcely forget, for he had lived up to his promise to make her very sorry. But she hadn't realised Nicky did.

'Why did you get into the car with him, Nick?' she asked.

His small forehead creased. 'He said you wanted me to, and he was nice before he put his hand over my mouth. Why did he do that, Lex?'

'He didn't mean to hurt you,' she evaded, reluctantly acknowledging the truth of it to herself. 'He was awfully sorry, and I promise he'll never do it again.'

Whether he was happy with her promise or not, she didn't know, because he suddenly lost interest in the subject and turned to the front of the balcony to lean his head between two rails of the ironwork. He surveyed the sea stretching far into the distance, face puckered with concentration.

'I can't see it, Lex,' he said eventually.

'What, Nick?'

'The island, of course,' he responded, as though there could hardly be any doubt as to what he was referring. 'It was only that much on the map,' he made a small gap between his thumb and forefinger, 'but that means miles and miles, doesn't it?'

'I expect so,' she agreed quietly. 'Nick, are you very disappointed about Daddy and the island?'

He didn't give her a direct answer, but there was a quiver to his bottom lip as he muttered, 'Maybe it was a dream like you said, Lex.'

And maybe not, Alex thought, wincing at the wistful note in Nicky's voice.

'Why don't we go and ask the man?' she forced out, and called herself all kinds of fool for even adding, 'He's bound to know because he was a very close friend of your daddy's.'

'*He* was?' he repeated sceptically.

Andros Kontos had obviously made a very bad impression on his nephew, so why change it? No reason. Alex looked past Nicky to that expanse of bright azure sea and again felt the impact of their surroundings on senses accustomed to the city.

Perhaps all that beauty made one lightheaded, for when she focused back on the little boy, she found herself admitting, 'Yes, Nicky, he was. In fact, he's your daddy's brother.'

His downturned mouth told her he remained unimpressed, and she almost laughed. What had she been expecting? She wasn't sure. But whatever her vague fears had been, they soon became real ones, as Nicky concluded, 'That makes him my uncle, doesn't it?—just like you're my aunt,' and Alex saw the repercussions of any similar remark.

'Listen, Nicky, do you think you could pretend to the man that...' she hesitated, feeling more shady than ruthless, '... that I'm your mother, not just your aunt?'

And felt no better after Nicky, having given it a moment's solemn consideration, made it simple for her.

'You are sort of now, Lex, aren't you? It wouldn't just be pretend, would it?'

'No. No, it wouldn't,' she reassured him, hearing the anxious note in his question, and was torn between smiling and weeping when he beamed his pleasure at the idea.

'Should I call you Mummy, then, 'stead of Lex?' he asked next.

'It doesn't matter, pet, as long as you...' she wavered, changing her mind about going deeper into explanations that might confuse and worry Nicky. She would have to trust to luck that Andros Kontos would refrain from giving him the third degree about their life in England—hadn't he already declared himself un-interested?—and Nicky, in turn, wouldn't say anything she couldn't cover up. '... As long as you know how much I love you, Nicky,' she finished, tilting his face to give him a light kiss.

'Love you too, Lex . . . Mum,' he tried out as they re-entered the house, and giggled at its unfamiliarity, although in the last couple of years his aunt had figured more prominently in his life than anybody else. He had loved his mother but, in truth, he loved Alex more.

On their arrival downstairs, they found Andros at a table in the shade of the lower balcony. He rose at their approach, held a chair out for Alex, and put away the correspondence he had been perusing. Breakfast passed in silence, Alex ignoring him and Nicky following suit.

'Have you told him?' The words were thrown across the table at her, more accusation than question.

Alex drew in a calming breath. Feigning ignorance, she murmured, 'I've told Nicky that you've kindly asked us to stay for a few days' holiday, yes.'

He would have to have been dull-witted not to discern the sarcasm dripping from her sweet response. He wasn't—his dark thunderous stare told her as much as their eyes clashed.

'That was not what I meant,' he said in icily restrained tones. 'But I think, Miss Saunders, you've given me my answer.'

Miss Saunders—how pompous it was beginning to sound!—knew precisely what he had meant and that he patently didn't believe she'd told Nicky the truth.

Remembering her own surprise at the boy's lack of reaction at suddenly gaining an uncle, she could understand how Andros had arrived at that conclusion.

Unfortunately she could also construe his anger as a measure of how much he cared about *Nicky's* opinion. Only one winner, she reminded herself sharply. But it didn't do any good, for notions of right and wrong overruled a more pragmatic approach.

'Nicky,' she coaxed softly, touching the boy's arm, 'why don't you ask your uncle about the island?'

Eyes shifting nervously to the man and then quickly back to Alex, he mumbled, 'Don't want to, Lex.'

She supposed she could have derived some satisfac-

tion as Andros's black brows drew together in a near
pained expression before he astounded her with a stiff
apology of, 'It appears I have misjudged the situation.'

Instead she compensated for the boy's embarrassing
rejection, 'I'm afraid he's very shy with strangers.'

It earned her a quick mystified frown, as he clearly
wondered what she was playing at. Alex wasn't too
certain herself.

'Did Theo tell you about the island?' he asked, still
scrutinising Alex's expression.

'He told Chris a little before he left,' she said, a shade
carelessly.

His eyes narrowed. 'They were good friends, this
Chris and my brother?'

'Very,' she confirmed, and understanding the contempt behind the question, fuelled it with an insolent,
'As you know, they had some *shared* interests.'

'Be careful, Miss Saunders.'

'Of what?' she challenged, forgetting their audience
for a second.

He did not. 'I would bear in mind before you make
any more rash remarks that the boy will not always be
present as protection.'

Alex was prevented from replying to this threat by
the return of the driver, who had discarded his jacket
in favour of a cook's apron. He beamed a grin at
Nicky, shyly returned, and then at Alex. But the smile
faded as Kontos stood up and began to speak in
rapid Greek.

Too quick for Alex to follow in detail—she presumed
him to be explaining his version of the circumstances.
The young driver confined his replies to yes and no,
plainly in awe of his employer.

Andros's switch to English was abrupt and he made
no attempt to change his tone from that of a master
used to ordering around his servants.

'I am returning to Athens to clear up our little
problem. You will tell the boy he should accompany
Mario to the pool. We need some words in private.'

Alex hesitated, but Nicky asked eagerly, 'Can I go, Lex?'

'If you want, but don't fall in the water,' she warned, resigning herself to being left alone with his uncle.

Taking it as permission, Nicky dashed excitedly from the table towards the pool, while Andros Kontos barked an order for Mario to follow him.

Then more slowly he said, 'He is like Theo in his recklessness,' and dazed Alex with the sudden indulgence in his tone. Shifting his gaze back to her, he added, 'Or maybe like his mother.'

'Of course some people never act on impulse,' Alex rallied.

Anticipating a return of his annoyance, he confounded her by admitting drily, 'Almost never—this morning things were moving a little fast, don't you agree?' But if it was an invitation to be reasonable, Alex's strained nerves refused to accept it.

'I hardly think that was my fault,' she snapped indignantly. 'I didn't ask to be kidnapped ... But maybe I would be good enough to forget what you've done if you take us to the airport and give me some money back,' she conceded with a haughty air.

He seemed uninterested in her offer, as he strolled away to the end of the balcony and looked down towards the pool. She followed him there, and for a moment they both stared at the little boy already dangling his legs over the water's edge.

When he turned to face her again, the Greek's derisive words destroyed any pleasure in the scene. 'Your act of outraged innocence seems singularly out of place in the repertoire of a blackmailer, Miss Saunders.'

She'd give him outraged innocence! Blackmailer! Alex flared, as she spluttered nearly speechless, 'Why, you ... you ...' and her hand rose reflexively to wipe the supercilious sneer from his face.

But this time he was ready for her. 'The act gets better every second,' he drawled. Desperately Alex tried to twist her hand out of the hard fingers that had intercepted the slap. But he captured her other wrist with a humiliating ease and gripped both rigidly in front of him, before he scoffed, 'Only I wouldn't try that again. Since I am a barbarian, my veneer of civilisation is rather thin.'

Alex continued to twist and pull away, but in the end his scornful laughter at her futile struggle to free herself, and her blinding resentment at the rough male bullying, incited her to use the most primitive of weapons in attack: she sank small sharp teeth into one of his hands.

His laughter died instantly, stifled on a note of surprise and pain, with only the sound of erratic, angry breathing to break the stunned silence as he shoved her at arms' length and all movement suspended.

Then his hands slowly released hers to clamp down on her shoulders, and, paralysed by the crazy notion she had asked for anything that was about to happen to her, Alex shut her eyes against his piercing stare.

And all she was aware of was long fingers curling round her neck, at first almost caressing, lightly forcing her head up. Sure he intended to throttle her, for a second she stopped breathing of her own accord. But the smell of tobacco and tangy cologne suddenly filled her nostrils and her eyes flickered open just as his black head descended to blot out air and light.

It was a kiss of punishment, savage and insulting, and had nothing whatever to do with love or lovemaking. Ended on her first sob of fright, Alex found herself trembling against the railing where he had pushed her. Eyes enormous with shock, she fingered lips bruised with the imprint of his mouth, incapable of coherent thought or speech.

Andros had no such problem. 'Next time, Miss Saunders, I suggest you take me at my word!' he bit out, before rounding on his heel and walking off with total victory.

CHAPTER FIVE

'HE's tall, isn't he?' Nicky suddenly remarked from nowhere as he toyed with his lunch.

'Who?' Alex muttered distractedly.

'The Man,' he said, giving the words capital letters.

Who else? Alex sighed to herself.

'Will I be that big when I'm grown up?' Nicky continued.

'Not if you don't eat your lunch, that's for certain,' she said in a tone that told him to concentrate on his food.

During the morning, Nicky had been making up for his earlier lack of interest in his new uncle. One more reference, however, she wasn't sure if she could take without yelling or weeping or something equally dramatic.

Being the girl she was, her sense of humiliation had long outlasted her fright. Hours later her mind was still preoccupied with things she could have said or done to alter the outcome of that dreadful scene.

Not that she *should* retract any of her statements. His kidnapping of them was quite outrageous, and she was relatively innocent, save for some minor fabrications forced on her by circumstances. Certainly she didn't deserve the term blackmailer. She hadn't accepted his bribe to hand over Nicky, had she? The money he had removed from her purse came into a different category. From any angle, she had the right to react to his sarcasm.

Oh yes, she could justify everything to herself. Even if plain good sense ought to have made her heed Andros's earlier warnings. What was that expression?—'might was right'—and hadn't he enjoyed showing her with mortifying ease that he had the upper hand in that direction, brute that he was.

Everything, yes, except her own violent reaction, she decided ruefully. How could she have done it? She felt so absurdly bad about it now, as though she should be wearing a sign round her neck with the warning, 'Beware of the girl, she bites'.

'Finished, Nick?' she asked, snapping out of her reverie.

He pushed his plate away. 'Can we go to the pool again, Lex?'

The fascination the pool held had not diminished, although he had not been in it yet. He wasn't a very good swimmer and there was no shallow end. Alex herself didn't have a bathing costume.

'It's very hot,' she wavered, inclined to stay under the shade of the table umbrella.

'I think it's nice.'

'Very well then,' she gave way. Indeed Nicky seemed to be bearing up to the heat much better than she was. Her clothes were sticking to her back and there was a fine film of perspiration on her forehead. She would have dearly loved a dip in the pool to cool off.

'It's a super place, isn't it?' Nicky enthused as they sat side by side, their legs kicking cool water.

'Yes, lovely,' she agreed with sinking spirits.

'Do you think The Man can swim?' Nicky asked guilelessly.

'You've changed your tune,' she said, striving not to sound cross. After all, he wasn't *trying* to depress her. 'I thought you didn't like him.'

He hunched his shoulders. 'Don't know him yet ... You were right, though, Lex,' he said next, off on another tangent.

She was? 'I have been known to be,' she laughed back. 'But about what in particular, kiddo?'

'He does like you,' he supplied as though it was clear as day.

It wasn't. 'Who, Nick?'

'The Man, 'course.'

His patient tone told her she was being slow, and

maybe she was. Too slow even to guess how he had
gathered this latest impression. It was almost funny.

Almost, until Nicky supported his claim with a
knowing, 'He did kiss you, so he must like you.'

And what could she say and not destroy such
precious naïvety? That a kiss could be a brutal
punishment was outside his scope. Till today—outside
hers as well. It had been a rude awakening she wasn't
about to share.

'Yes, of course he does,' she said heartily, as though
Andros Kontos was one of her biggest fans. 'I said so,
didn't I?'

Her bright smile was returned. At all costs, Nicky
wasn't going to be made a battleground. He went back
to splashing the water with his feet, fortunately losing
interest in the topic.

'I'm sorry you can't go in, Nick.'

'I could loan you my shorts,' he suggested helpfully.

She laughed, 'They're a bit small, I think.'

'Couldn't you . . .?'

'No, I couldn't!' she retorted smartly, glancing
behind them and receiving a broad grin from their ever-
present shadow. Not even for Nicky was she about to
strip down to bra and briefs in front of their
obnoxiously friendly guard. 'Why don't you ask him if
he can swim?' she suggested with a shade of irony.

'I did,' Nicky admitted.

He would have! He loved swimming. Wasn't he
prepared to forgive the Man his earlier transgressions
for the chance of practising that clumsy dog-paddle?

'And he can't,' Alex surmised.

'Dunno.' He pulled a rueful grimace. 'He talks
strange.'

No English, she presumed. So much for any fanciful
notions of enlisting the young man's help to get away!
Her basic Greek didn't stretch to the smooth talking
she sensed would be necessary—she hadn't missed his
'knee-bending' to Andros. Still, it just might extend to
asking him if he could swim.

Stretching up, she approached the young man. Nicky trailed behind her. In faltering Greek Alex enquired, 'Can you swim with the boy?'

'He doesn't understand, Lex,' Nicky pointed out the obvious, while the driver shrugged expressively at her repeated request.

She could see she had at least one word wrong and she suspected she was, in fact, saying something rather rude. Their guard was having great difficulty suppressing the laughter that quirked the corners of his mouth.

'Doesn't understand,' he mimicked with a smile.

She sighed heavily. 'It doesn't matter,' she resumed in English. Trust Andros Kontos to leave her with a guard she couldn't even talk to!

Fortunately the young man was not so ready to give up and Alex literally did a doubletake when he offered, *'Parliamo Italiano?'*

Did she speak Italian? It seemed like a miracle—too good to be true.

'Do you?' she returned in Italian, rather obtusely she realised afterwards. He would hardly be suggesting it as an alternative if he didn't.

'My parents came from Italy,' he announced in his native language and with another of his wide grins. 'My name is Mario Amborelli.'

Alex wondered if the hot sun was beginning to affect her reasoning powers. Why in heaven's name hadn't it occurred to her earlier that Mario was not a Greek name? Eagerly she translated her question into fluent Italian—one of the languages in her degree course—and if anything the young man was more delighted than she was. Mario apparently was as fond of talking as he was of smiling. Alex did not object.

'Where's he going?' Nicky demanded when he eventually bounded off towards the house.

'To fetch, would you believe, a bikini so we can go swimming, kiddo,' she said with a smug grin.

'Whoopee!' he cried, immediately tearing off his tee-shirt.

'Not so fast, buster!' She caught him mid-flight. 'You have to wait till he comes back.'

'Wish he'd hurry up,' he complained, giggling as she tickled his squirming body.

'Impatient child!' she explained. 'He's only just gone.'

But Mario was back almost immediately, changed into swimming trunks and carrying the skimpiest bikini Alex had ever laid eyes on. While he supervised Nicky, she hurried inside to change. And for the second time that day, she found herself studying her reflection in a mirror.

Was she a prude or was it really one tiny inch from being totally indecent? she asked herself with a critical eye. A bit of both, she concluded as she tried to hitch up the halterneck top to cover more of her breasts, looking fuller in this scrap of black cloth, and tied the drawstrings even tighter.

It was the sort of costume designed for sunbathing rather than swimming, and definitely not the kind of thing she would have chosen herself. Still, there wasn't any alternative if she wanted to take a swim. She hadn't asked why Mario was so certain he could find her a bikini in the villa. She could imagine.

Self-conscious, she wore her shirt as a makeshift beachrobe until she was at the pool's edge. But she soon relaxed in Mario's company. If she caught him looking at her as she poised to dive in, his eyes slid away in obvious embarrassment and when they eventually left the water, he waited to be invited to sit with them on the sun-loungers at the far end from the villa.

Gradually he became talkative again, but it took Alex less than an hour (during which she lost count of how often 'Signor Kontos says' prefixed his sentences) to discount a direct appeal for the young man's help.

Apparently Mario had a mother, a Greek stepfather and a little half-brother, all of whom also relied on Andros Kontos for their living. And apart from his near reverence for his employer, it was astonishingly evident that the simple, boyish Italian wasn't even aware he was playing gaoler. He was the attentive servant, providing a steady supply of iced fruit drinks; the conscientious guardian of their welfare, no sooner asking if Alex found the sun a little strong than rushing off to fetch a giant yellow sunshade, and later carrying an exhausted Nicky inside the house for a nap; so respectful she wondered what on earth Andros Kontos had told him.

He too seemed surprised by her ignorance about the Kontos family, but he was easily led on the subject. She learned that far from the close Greek family she had visualised in the background, there was only Theo's brother left—his father having died in the same accident, his mother a short year later. But if she was up against just one individual, it wasn't comforting to discover him to be the owner of a chain of hotels that stretched from the Greek Islands to the Spanish coast, or that her 'barbarian' had been educated at Oxford University, of all places.

At first it made her feel despondent, and then cross with herself for being so. She might not have his money, but that didn't mean she was helpless. She should be doing something. For certain, Kontos wasn't wasting the afternoon in lazing around a swimming pool. She *had* to do something. But what?

Mario's gangling frame appearing at her side by the pool encouraged rather than gave her the idea. Her smile was beguiling as she tilted her head back and patted the space beside her, murmuring, 'Come and sit by me, Mario.'

Obediently he sank down on the tiling, and Alex forced herself into the role, confident she could handle him. Drawing one leg out of the water in a slow graceful movement, she gave him what she hoped was a sultry look. It worked—inasmuch as his eyes unconsciously strayed to widen appreciatively on her shapely figure—but his blatant stare was quickly followed by a fierce blush.

'How old are you, Mario?' she asked, frowning.

'Nineteen,' he admitted with reluctance.

She should be ashamed of herself, Alex thought, for even trying a corny *femme fatale* act on the boy. Not only was he two years her junior but, if she was any judge, as inexperienced as herself.

There was a long awkward moment of silence between them until Mario suddenly dared to look at her again and blurted out, 'I think you are very beautiful, *signora*.'

'Thank you,' Alex acknowledged coolly. Poor Mario seemed to be catching on late, but she had no inclination to pursue it. Instead she said outright, 'I'd like to go to the nearest village. How far is it?'

'Ten kilometres,' he answered automatically, 'but we have no car and Signor Kontos says . . .'

'He says?' she prompted.

'That you must be prevented from walking in the sun too much,' he repeated his instructions innocently. 'You are not used to it, you see. Signor Kontos says he will be back soon and then he will take you.'

Alex managed to return Mario's apologetic smile. What else could she do, other than cry with frustration? It wasn't his fault he was so easy to manipulate, so unaware of what had really happened that morning. But another 'Signor Kontos says', and she knew she would scream aloud.

She dived back in the water.

Even from a distance, she had appeared to be talking to the boy, smiling at him with the same charm she used on the child. It had not occurred to him that she would know any Greek—perhaps stupid of him not to consider that his brother might have taught her some of their language. But his mind was already stretched trying to make sense of the whole affair.

Theo had been a little wild as a young man. That was why their father had sent him to England where he would not be able to trade on his position as son of the wealthy Kontos family to attract so many women and

neglect his studies. Andros himself had been despatched
ten years earlier to Oxford for much the same reason,
along with the prestige his self-educated father had seen
attached to the famous English university. In truth, like
Theo, he had not found being in a foreign country on a
very small allowance had prevented him from enjoying
the more permissive atmosphere in England. But *he*
wouldn't have shared that girl—any girl, he amended
angrily—with another man. He had too much pride.
Apparently Theo hadn't.

After a meeting with his lawyer, Andros had spent
the day thinking, of the past as well as the previous
twenty-four hours, and coming up with a picture of the
way things had been for his brother. It was not pretty.

He remembered the last time he had seen Theo, just
back from England and entreating him to intercede
with their old-fashioned father, to explain that he
couldn't possibly ever go through with that long-
standing arrangement with their second cousin Helena.
He was in love with someone else. Andros had not
taken that particularly seriously at the time, but he had
sympathised. The elder Kontos had been putting a great
deal of pressure on Theo from the moment of his return
to abandon the hotel management course that seemed
to be requiring an inordinate time to pass, and settle
down in Greece with the pretty but dull Helena. Theo,
always intimidated by their father's quick-tempered
rages, was greatly distressed by the idea. Then Andros
had persuaded his younger brother that their father
would think more of him if he did his own fighting.
Now he wondered what had been said on that fatal
flight back to the island.

Had Theo meant to marry Alex Saunders? For the
child's sake, he could appreciate, but Theo had declared
himself in love with her, their relationship already four
years old, Andros calculated. In love with a woman he
had to share with another man. Somehow Andros knew
it would have been like that—the English girl dictating
her terms, fractioning her life between the two males.

With her pride, it would not have been otherwise, for all that the letter from the man Chris had given the impression she was the one badly treated by Theo. But then he had been in love with her too—how else could he have looked after her and another man's child?

It was not the sort of love Andros could understand. With no trace of shame, the girl had claimed the men to have been friends. If he had been Theo and in love with the girl, he would have wanted to kill any other man who laid so much as a finger on her. Or more likely killed the girl who let him, he decided on a bitter note, recalling Alex Saunders' talent for evoking a fury that made him want to hurt her, to crush all that wayward wanton spirit out of her.

He watched as she did another elegant turn at the end of the pool nearest his vantage point of the upper balcony. Eyes moving with the slender figure smoothly cleaving through the water, he noticed he was not her only spectator. Mario was still sitting at the poolside, grinning broadly whenever she reached his end of the water and stopped for breath. He had told the boy to look after her; Mario appeared to be taking the order very literally. The lad's interest should have pleased him. It fitted in so well with the advice his lawyer had given him.

He had told Stephanos the story from beginning to end, and his friend had presumed on their long acquaintance to tell him what a bloody fool he was for snatching the girl in broad daylight, and to all but agree when Andros had asked sarcastically would it have been any better if he had done it in the dead of night. Lawyers dealt in cases, not moralities.

Stephanos had then gone on to outline practicalities. He could attempt to buy the woman off with more money, assuming her ostensible rejection of his first offer was a tactical ploy; Andros himself was not so sure it would be that easy, not any more. Or he could take her to court and undoubtedly lose if he couldn't come up with some hard facts that would support his desperation to remove his nephew from her influence. After all, circumstances made her seem the one to have been taken advantage of by a wealthy Greek boy.

Andros saw his point, but he had assured his friend that less of a victim than Alex Saunders he was unlikely to meet. Yet when Stephanos had asked him what the girl was like, he ended up ducking the question with a wry 'indescribable'. For she was a mass of contradictions, this girl—stunningly insolent one moment, shocked and outraged by his retaliatory behaviour the next. Which was real? The first he had surmised when he had reluctantly given his agreement to sending an agent to London to gain more details on her past.

Meanwhile he had to treat her with kid gloves—to all appearances, a guest in his home, borne out by her coming to Greece at his invitation—and hope they could rake up enough dirt to satisfy a Greek court that she was unfit to be the child's guardian.

Yes, he should have been pleased at Mario's evident fascination. In time the girl would surely grow bored by her confinement, and if the Italian boy was induced to become bolder . . .

So why should he feel decidedly nauseated by the idea? He had to face facts. From any approach, it was going to be a nasty business, he realised, as he turned to go back inside the villa.

The little boy had kicked off his light covering sheet, but his arms still clutched a dilapidated teddy bear. His body looked thin and frail, his face puckered vulnerably in sleep. Both endorsed Andros's view that a woman like Alex Saunders could not be a proper mother. Yet he plainly adored her—another contradiction.

Reinforced as the boy suddenly woke and catching sight of him, asked immediately, 'Where's Lex?'

Well, at least he hadn't screamed the house down, Andros mused with small consolation. 'She's just outside, Nicholas. Swimming in the pool.'

The boy sat up in the bed and studied him curiously, before saying, 'Lex calls me Nicky.'

'All right, Nicky,' the man agreed. 'And you always call your mother Lex?' The child looked wary for a second or two. Had he detected his disapproval for the girl's lack of convention?

' 'Course,' Nicky replied with the same forthrightness. 'That's her name, A-*lex*-and-ra.'

A silly question on his part, he was made to feel, and he searched for something else to say, to keep the boy talking. As Alex Saunders had implied earlier, he knew next to nothing about children.

'Lex says you're my uncle,' Nicky supplied when the man stayed silent. 'What do I call you?'

'Uncle Andros? . . . Ros if you like.' The man's face lost its grimness as he gave the child a smile. It was shyly returned. 'I'm sorry I hurt you in the car, Nicky.'

The little boy gave a forgiving shrug. 'Lex says you didn't mean to and you won't do it again,' he repeated with absolute faith.

'Then Lex is right,' Andros confirmed aloud, but wondered what the girl was playing at. He had been expecting his nephew's earlier hostility to have grown since this morning, fostered in his absence. He understood Alex Saunders less and less.

'She always is,' Nicky replied in all seriousness before pointing at the parcel the man had laid in front of him. 'What's that?'

'It's a present.' The boy made no move towards opening the brown wrapping paper until Andros added encouragingly, 'For you.'

'I'm not allowed to take things from strangers,' Nicky stated, his face a struggle between conscience and temptation.

Andros tipped the balance by pointing out, 'I'm not really a stranger, Nicky. I'm your uncle, no?'

'Yes,' the boy smiled back. Problem solved, he reached for the parcel.

The man watched him tearing off the paper and saw the excitement reflected in his eyes, but heard an echo of Alex's words—'expensive presents, spoiling'. It lingered accusingly as the child drew the intricately-made toy out of its box, and his small face radiated silent wonder. Forcibly Andros had to reject any truth in the girl's claim. The present was his apology for hurting his nephew earlier. He had no intention of spoiling the child in the future. He just needed some advantages now.

Nicky accepted Andros's help to get dressed and offered him his hand as they descended the stone steps to the pool. Insisting on holding on to his new, prized possession, he pulled his uncle along in his hurry to show off the toy.

Mario alerted Alex to their arrival with, 'See, I told you he would not be long.' He extended his hand and she barely registered his arm steadying her at the waist after he had helped her out of the water.

Her eyes were fixed rigidly on Andros, still dressed in a sombre grey suit, and the boy at his side, clutching the toy to his small chest.

'Isn't it lovely, Lex?' Nicky said proudly.

Yes, the model sailing yacht was lovely, but Alex couldn't trust herself to speak. She nodded, her eyes going back to Kontos with a fierce glare telling him exactly how she viewed the present. He held her stare for a few seconds, before he glanced at Mario to toss him a set of car keys and with some brisk orders dismiss him for the day.

'How do I work it?' Nicky demanded, distracting her attention. He had placed the boat in the water and in one hand held a slim plastic control panel.

She didn't believe it—an electronic model! On second thoughts, she did. A perfect replica of a rich man's toy in miniature, it was just the sort of present a millionaire would buy.

'Why don't you ask your kind generous uncle?' she suggested with an acid sweetness.

Andros's eyes narrowed. 'It isn't like that.'

But Alex hadn't waited to hear his reply or watch him give patient instructions to the little boy. So much for her determination to say nothing inflammatory to Andros, to say nothing full stop. She had to get out of here!

Through a gap in the foliage that surrounded the pool, she traced the road, disappearing and reappearing as it wound down the hillside. There was no other villa in sight, confirming what Mario had already told her. Few people could afford to build so high. There was no path directly down the hill either that would cut the distance to the village.

A voice behind her mirrored her thoughts. 'It's a long way down. Too far for the child to walk.'

Did he have to sound so smug, so sure of himself? 'I know that. What do you think kept me here—your tame watchdog?' she jeered as she wheeled round to face Andros.

'Mario? No, I don't suppose you'd let him stop you,' he allowed, eyes catching hers again. 'In fact, you appear to have that situation under control. How much Greek do you know?'

'Not much.'

'Enough, it seems,' he remarked dryly.

Enough for what? Alex frowned, but decided not to ask. Instinct told her to conceal her knowledge of Italian.

She glanced away, checking on Nicky who, face down on the tiles, was studying the boat skimming over the water—this way and that when he operated the controls.

Turning back, she discovered that Andros did not share Mario's reticence. She had forgotten how skimpy her bikini was, but his dark eyes moving slowly over her gave her cause to remember. It could hardly be described as undressing—the bikini didn't leave that much to the imagination—but his eyes were certainly thorough. When they eventually travelled back to her face, there was no question who was embarrassed this time.

'It's . . . it's not mine,' Alex found herself defending,

and then stuttering on, even more foolishly, 'I mean—
it's yours. At least, I mean—I didn't have a costume, so
Mar . . . I borrowed this one from the house.'

'You can keep it. I think it fits you *slightly* better
than me, don't you?' His gaze dipped momentarily to
the swell of high, full breasts exposed by the brief
swimsuit. 'You look good in the bikini. Very tempting,
in fact,' he drawled.

Alex didn't have to work very hard at guessing who
she was supposed to be tempting. Assuredly not him,
still dressed in a suit and looking inhumanly cool in the
stifling heat which must account for the fresh
perspiration breaking out on her skin.

'Spare me that routine,' she muttered aloud, and at
his bland stare, expanded exasperatedly, 'You appear to
have a much higher opinion of my attractions than I
have, Mr Kontos. You left Mario to watch over me. So
he watched. And that's it!'

He caught her arm as she made to pass him. 'I saw
the two of you talking. For a girl who knows very little
Greek, you seemed to be *communicating* rather well.'

She sighed heavily. 'If you must know, I can speak
Italian.'

'Really?'

Alex gave him a rapid sample and then enquired at his
obvious incomprehension. 'Would you like a translation?'

'Not particularly,' he said, anticipating its rudeness.
'So what were you and Mario talking about?'

'Mario talked at great and boring length about his
favourite subject.'

'Which is?' he queried with heavy patience.

'You!' Alex flipped back, completing the insult.

But Andros threw back his head and laughed, damn
him! She shot him a withering glance which hadn't the
desired effect either—if anything, it increased his
enjoyment.

'You have spirit, Alex Saunders,' he observed in
deeply amused tones. 'It is a pity we didn't meet in
other circumstances.'

'Why?' demanded Alex, and then instinctively flinched as he trailed a light finger down her cheek in an insolent caress.

'No matter,' he dismissed, and left Alex standing, staring after his back and wondering what he had meant. She couldn't envisage any circumstances in which she would wish to know the man, for all his wealth and physical attraction. Undeniable, she conceded, if you liked tall, dark macho types. She didn't! She liked . . . well, she wasn't quite sure what she liked, but definitely not him.

Nonetheless she covertly watched him when he reappeared some minutes later dressed in dark swimming trunks. She had thought his expensively tailored suit might have hidden a businessman's waistline. She had been wrong.

Unclothed, his body had the same lean, athletic grace, from broad muscular shoulders and chest to long sinewy legs. Yet all that male perfection only served to increase Alex's anger against 'The Man'.

She had to get out of here, she repeated to herself for the umpteenth time, as though it was a charm that would suddenly spirit them down the hillside to the village. And then what? He had their money and her return plane ticket. She still had her passport, so she presumed she could go to the British Embassy in Athens. That was what people did when they were stranded in a foreign country, wasn't it? So, if they could get to the village, then somehow to Athens, and be flown back home, courtesy of the British government, then what?

Back in London, jobless and homeless, they would have come full circle. In the light of her promise to keep Nicky out of the Home, Alex almost believed they were better off here.

'Where are you going?' His call interrupted her thoughts as she found herself approaching the steps at the side of the house.

She turned and saw him haul himself out of the water

to stand hands on hips at its edge. The last time she had looked, he had been covering the pool with a fast crawl, back and forth in ritualistic exercise.

She could scarcely tell him she was going inside to think, to get out of the sun that seemed to be affecting her power to do so rationally.

'I have to wash some clothes,' she said on the spur of the moment. 'I didn't bring much,' she added, although truthfully they each had a week's change of clothing.

'If you give me the boy's measurements, I'll get some tomorrow,' he offered straightaway. 'And you are . . .'

'No, thank you,' she interrupted his sizing appraisal of her figure.

'Why not?' he demanded.

He had to be kidding! 'What's that expression?' she muttered rhetorically, ' "Beware the Greeks when they come bearing gifts".'

'It wasn't like that,' he repeated, intercepting her bitter glance at the little boy, still absorbed in his new toy. 'I felt bad about hurting him. You understand?'

Evidently very little. The sun *must* be getting to her. It sounded remarkably as if he was justifying himself— to her, of all people!

'Alex?'

This time she didn't let his call detain her, although she was startled by his sudden use of her first name. She reached her room just before the tears came. Absurd, stupid, weakening tears streaming down her face as she flung herself on the bed, overwhelmed by the whole awful situation.

Why shouldn't he buy Nicky presents? drummed through her head as she cried her misery out. For all her earlier remarks about spoiling, she knew the real reason she objected, and it was as shabby as the cast-off clothes the boy wore. Andros Kontos could afford them, she couldn't—and never would. Damn him!

CHAPTER SIX

NICKY soon turned dinner into a less than silent affair as he fast lost any shyness with Andros, and fired question after question about the island where the Kontos family had lived. Alex was glad when his eyelids began to droop and his uncle Ros—how quickly the boy had become used to the name—scooped him out of his chair up to bed.

She cleared the table on the terrace and went to the kitchen. Setting cups and saucers on the tray, she wondered how he took his coffee. In the end she placed two jugs on the tray, a choice of milk or cream, and a bowl of brown sugar.

She explored the kitchen while she waited for the percolator to boil. Stone-tiled and with white-plastered walls, it was finished in dark oak, concealing behind wooden fascias every labour-saving device imaginable, and yet like the rest of the villa more stylish than ostentatious. If it wasn't a paradox, expensive but simple.

Having discovered a dishwasher Alex stacked the dinner plates and glasses inside, and switched on, praying she wouldn't hear the sound of broken crockery as she selected a button. It was her sole contribution to the meal Andros had prepared while she brooded in her room.

When she went through with the coffee, he was seated back at the terrace table, smoking a cigarette and staring out to sea. It was not yet dusk, the air still pleasantly warm. He rose as Alex approached and took the tray from her hands.

He poured the coffee and offered her a cigarette from a gold case. She would have liked to refuse, but if ever she needed one to soothe her nerves, it was now. He flicked his lighter, and the politeness of his gesture caused her to stifle a laugh at its irony—the gentleman kidnapper?

But then perhaps that was the general idea, to lull her sensibilities, she speculated, as he broke the lengthening silence to ask her if she would like more coffee.

'No, thank you,' she murmured aloud, and immediately wondered if she wasn't falling for it. Tired of waiting for him to relay his plans, she cleared her throat and bluntly said what was in her mind. 'Do you think you could skip the gracious host act? When we're alone, at any rate.'

His eyes lifted from pouring his own coffee, hardening at her tone but definitely wary. 'I'm not sure what you mean, Miss Saunders.'

He had returned to 'Miss Saunders'—good!

'You've already convinced Mario that I'm here willingly and I've been obliged to give that impression to Nicky, so why not settle for that?'

'Why not?' he granted after slanting her an assessing look. 'Perhaps I should have asked your advice and saved myself a trip to my lawyer.'

So that's was where he had been, clearing up their little problem. Only it hadn't been cleared, had it? Otherwise she wouldn't be sitting here if he was certain of Nicky's custody.

'I gave you my advice this morning,' she pointed out.

He nodded, his expression unreadable even when he murmured back, 'Rather forcefully, as I remember.'

It might have been intentional, his raising of the hand she had bitten to draw on his cigarette, but Alex was horrified to see she had actually broken the skin, however tiny the cut between thumb and forefinger.

'I'm sorry. I didn't mean to be so ...' she began impulsively, but the rest of her words lodged in her throat as a mocking light entered his eyes.

'So?' he prompted softly, and was awarded a scowl as savage as her bite had been.

Was he trying to make her lose her temper? He hadn't been exactly gentle with her.

'*I'm* trying to be reasonable,' she said, although she failed to quite sound it.

His sardonic look suggested it made a change, but he said, 'I too regret my behaviour . . . some of it, at least.' As an apology it was less than convincing, especially with his eyes resting for a second on the sullen set of her mouth. 'You can be very provocative, Alex Saunders,' he accused, still in the same mocking tone.

'I thought it might turn out to be all my fault.' She matched his dryness and wished she hadn't when he laughed softly. She wasn't there to entertain him in after-dinner conversation. 'So what now?' she asked shortly, and saw him shed his amused manner.

'I am willing to consider your advice in part.'

'You are?' she quizzed, not daring to hope for too much.

It was just as well, for he excused himself and came back within seconds holding a piece of paper. Before he placed it in front of her she knew what it was, but she couldn't help herself gasping at the figure stated on the bank draft. Her eyes flew to his. They were coldly measuring her response.

'What are you doing?' he demanded, astounded at her next action.

Alex would have thought it was obvious as she continued to fold the cheque until it was the right shape.

Her aim was good. She did not wait to watch the paper aeroplane flutter down the hillside.

It would have been a perfect exit if it had been a play. Unfortunately it wasn't, and Andros had no hesitation in hauling her back from the outside stairs and bodily dragging her into the living room. Roughly he shoved her down on the couch.

'Don't move!' he shouted as she made to rise. 'And, for once, don't talk!'

She closed her mouth and *for once* obeyed. She didn't have much option with him towering over her, hands clenching and unclenching in angry fists, but there had been no instruction about the defiant blaze on her face as she tilted her head back.

For a long tense moment their gazes locked, each demanding that the other back down. Alex felt she had a right, more right, to be angry, and she had no intention of giving in. Only she did, completely losing her nerve at the hard ruthless glint in his dark eyes. She wasn't left doubting what might have happened, if she hadn't dropped her eyes in submission and shown her fear with the slight, shameful trembling of her body.

As his anger eventually broke, he said in a near groan, 'I swear—Alex, you are going to make me hurt you,' before he stalked to the drinks cabinet and slammed bottle and glass on its surface.

So what now? Alex thought, but this time she didn't say it out loud. Right at that precise second she was uncertain whether she could say anything without stuttering. It was bad enough that he had her frightened and worse that he knew it.

A full five minutes must have passed before he spoke again. Wordlessly he had placed a drink on the coffee table in front of her and flung himself down on the chair farthest from her. She sensed him sitting there, slowly recovering his temper. When she herself regained enough nerve to look at him directly, it was to find herself the object of his close scrutiny.

'Explain it to me,' he said at last, and waited. For what Alex hadn't the faintest idea, but she had no inclination to recommence warfare. Quietly she murmured back, 'I'm not sure what you mean.'

'All right, I'll give you my version,' he said, and went on to do so in the same deep, even tone.

'Your friend Chris writes to Theo asking him to take responsibility for the child. Meanwhile you place the boy in an orphanage. On receiving my letter, admittedly under the impression that it is from Theo, you bring the boy to Greece.

'Last night you accept my offer of money, but this morning you get up at the crack of dawn apparently to fly back to England. Caught out, you demand that I take you to the airport and give you money. Tonight I make an improved offer, and you indulge your humour at my expense.

'So where do we go from here, Miss Saunders?'

Again he waited, watching the indecision flitting across Alex's face. From his viewpoint she could see how it might look; but she wasn't going to give him any explanation. She couldn't even give one to herself, she admitted silently, and despaired at how things had grown so complicated in just twenty-four hours.

But certain that this was only the changing tactics of a quick-witted businessman, Alex said guardedly, 'You got us here. You tell me.'

And if it had been a chance to tell him the truth, she surely lost it as her caginess was mistaken for insolence.

'Very well, Miss Saunders, as you seem incapable of taking the situation seriously, I shall take you at your word,' he dictated coldly. 'Since it is not in the boy's interest to be separated from his mother too suddenly— and since I have no intention of giving up the right to offer him a decent life, we will effect a compromise.'

Alex rolled off her stomach to lie on her back. Like on that eventful morning now five days in the past, the curtains had been left undrawn and strong sunlight was spilling across the room. Flickering her eyes open, she felt that initial well-being of waking up to sunshine and spacious surroundings, and mused lazily, 'I could get used to this.'

Then, more alert, she pulled herself up against the cane bedrest. She *was* getting used to it, *too* used, she worried. Perhaps it was fortunate that today things were to change radically. For better or worse, she was uncertain, but more than a small part of her hoped it would be worse, their new situation—so intolerable, it would force her out of the dangerous lethargy that was gradually stealing over her.

She still didn't know quite how she had come to

agree to it—his compromise. Indeed, stunned by his suggestion, she couldn't remember that she'd said anything.

And now, today, they were leaving this lovely villa for the family home, which sounded even more remote, perched as it was on a rock barely four miles across.

'Compromise,' Alex repeated the word out loud, as though it would help her figure out what lay behind Andros's planning.

Why hadn't she just told the Man—God, she was at it now, giving him an exaggerated importance!—to go to hell, when he pointed out that as she was so obviously short of funds, she had little option but to fall in with his plans? Truce or not, she would once have had the nerve to do so, the pride to make her.

She was being sensible, she told herself firmly. For the moment she would accept her lack of alternative and play it day by day till ... till ... well, until their uneasy alliance inevitably fell apart and the hostilities resumed.

And then?

There was a light knock on her bedroom door, and readily Alex abandoned her speculations as Nicky enquired from the corridor if she was awake. It was a new habit that the child had acquired, this respecting of her privacy which would have been ridiculous in the tiny London flats in which they had lived.

She knew its origin. Consciously or not, he was picking up his uncle's impeccable manners. With a wry smile she went to open the door, not bothering to cover the short nightshirt she was wearing.

'Good morning, kiddo,' she said brightly, bending down to give the boy an affectionate kiss, but straightening when she noticed he was not alone in the corridor. Was he trying to catch her at a disadvantage? she wondered as once more she experienced the embarrassment of living so closely with a man who was not her husband, was not anything at all.

'We got you breakfast, Lex,' the boy stated proudly

as Alex's gaze dropped from the man's unshaven face to the tray he was carrying. 'I've been up hours, but Uncle Ros said I wasn't to dis . . . wake you.'

'Three quarters of an hour,' the man corrected with a smile in his voice. It disappeared when he acknowledged Alex. 'Good morning, Miss Saunders.'

'Good morning,' Alex echoed stiffly, looking anywhere but in the direction of those dark, perceptive eyes again and fighting the urge to do something about the neckline of her nightshirt that gashed deeply between the valley of her breasts. She stretched her arms for the tray. 'Thank you,' she continued the polite charade that had got them through the last few days in a semblance of harmony.

'My pleasure,' he murmured with a softly dry inflection that made her doubt it. Only when she made the mistake of raising challenging eyes back to him, she realised just what his 'pleasure' was meant to be. He was staring at the swell of one breast partly exposed to his lazy appreciation.

If he was trying to make her feel uncomfortable with that casual, almost detached interest, he was certainly succeeding! It rattled Alex and the tray she jerked out of his hands.

Not him, of course, for he added smoothly, 'Take your time about getting ready. We won't be leaving until the afternoon,' before sauntering off down the corridor with Nicky in tow.

He could still surprise her, she decided when she surveyed the tray of coffee and hot croissants. Not for a second did she believe he had carried breakfast up to her room to see what she looked like first thing in the morning, yet she couldn't fathom out his behaviour. She could imagine that the owner of the black bikini and the silky briefs forgotten in the back of a drawer would be expected to provide sustenance while her arrogant Greek master relaxed back in bed after a night of . . .

She imagined far too much! Alex gave herself a mental

shake and reached for the tray. She would eat his food and not go searching for the motivation in everything he did. Put it down to craziness—his—and learn to live with it in the unquestionably short time this arrangement would last.

She was dressed by the time Nicky returned, chattering on about an island he hadn't even seen outside his dreams. In all fairness to Andros, he hadn't tried to spoil Nicky or encourage the boy's interest—only answering his questions about the family home factually. In fact Alex had the strong impression that their move to Armina was to indulge Nicky's curiosity rather than out of a personal desire on Andros's part. Mario had told her that while his mother and stepfather were among the servants retained to upkeep the house on the small island, it was rare for their employer to visit the place. Alex supposed he preferred being nearer the capital.

'What about my boat?' Nicky asked as the second of the two borrowed cases was also filled.

'We'll put it back in its box and carry it separately,' she promised, removing the treasured toy from the pile of new shorts, tee-shirts and light jerseys. There had been no more expensive gifts other than the parcels of boy's clothing she had found on Nicky's bed the previous evening.

She fingered one of the soft towelling tops, striped blue and white and just the sort of thing she would have chosen herself. Glancing at the little boy still wearing one of his shabby, ill-fitting tee-shirts, she took the new one out of the case and a pair of cotton shorts to match.

'Why don't you change into these, Nick, before we go down?'

'They'll get dirty if I wear them,' he replied in all seriousness, intimidated by the very newness of the clothes, 'and Uncle Ros might get mad.'

'Don't be silly,' she chided mildly, pulling his present top over his head and replacing it with the striped one.

'He won't mind if you get them dirty. They're only clothes.'

Beautiful, smart clothes that instantly transformed him from near street urchin to that handsome cared-for appearance children of the wealthy always seemed to have, Alex thought as he finished dressing and she brought some order to his curling hair.

'He made me dress in my old clothes,' Nicky pointed out, still fretting over his uncle's possible reaction.

'I think he was waiting for me to choose what you should wear,' she gave the only explanation she could see and frowned over the perplexing man Andros Kontos was proving to be—one moment coldly outlining his proposals without the slightest consultation of her opinion, the next considering her feelings over the boy's new finery. At least that was how it appeared.

They went downstairs and Nicky settled in front of the lounge table with a colouring book while she went through to the kitchen. It had already formed a pattern in the evenings, his cooking and her washing up afterwards. In ways, for a rich man he lived very simply. She had contemplated in a madder moment offering to reverse the roles, but he cooked surprisingly well—far better than herself, she had to admit—so she concentrated on keeping the place tidy.

It was when she had finished and surveyed her effort with some satisfaction that she actually became conscious of the keys lying next to the coffee percolator, although she must have cleaned round them. She didn't need the Mercedes badge on the key ring to identify them. Andros must have left them there while he made breakfast.

'How careless of him,' she muttered, but her mind was halfway to another suspicion, for careless was the last thing she would have thought him.

She snatched up the keys, went to the kitchen door backing on to the steps leading to the road, and looked upwards. The fence gate was open, itself unusual, allowing her a glimpse of the long, sleek Mercedes parked hard against it.

Then she strolled around to the far end of the lower balcony, feeling no sense of urgency but a cold fury spreading over her while she watched Andros swimming back and forth, pausing between turns to raise his black head out of the water in a listening attitude.

As a baited trap, it was all too obvious for words.

Alex didn't waste many as she descended the short flight of steps from terrace to pool level and waited for him to complete his next length. She offered him a sweet smile after he tossed the wet hair out of his eyes, and it etched a surprised groove across his high forehead. When he seemed about to lever himself out of the pool, she extended an arm and opened her hand, palm upwards.

'Your keys,' she muttered scathingly, her false smile disappearing as she threw them towards the centre of the pool before marching back to the house.

Anger mingled with trepidation when she heard the peremptory knock on her bedroom door a short time later. She did not answer it. The door opened and closed very quietly. Out of the corner of her eye she saw Andros was now dressed in fine wool slacks and a blue cashmere sweater. The effect was both casual and elegant. She went on packing her own clothes, studiously ignoring him.

He came no further than the door, leaning his weight on its frame. He watched her so long without speaking, she wondered if she was in for one of his 'he-man' exhibitions. Well, she thought, as she dragged out the folding of her blouse, she didn't care!

Nevertheless she jumped when he eventually moved away from his leaning post to hover behind her shoulder.

'All right, I'm sorry,' he said very quietly—not what Alex had been expecting at all. She gave him marks for sounding sincere, none for being so.

'I'm sure you are,' she snapped back, lending her own interpretation to his words as she crushed the blouse into the suitcase and refused to look at him. In highly sarcastic tones, she went on, 'Perhaps you should have left me a few other subtle lures—like a bulging wallet, or maybe a road map with the route to Athens marked in red!'

He spun her round, but inexplicably he didn't seem angry, more interested in why she was. 'You're mad because I insulted your intelligence, yes?' he asked, eyes narrowed on her tight furious mouth.

'Why else?' she spat back. 'Don't think it bothers me that you don't trust me an inch!' she exclaimed bitterly.

'I wouldn't be so presumptuous,' he said calmly—too calmly for Alex's liking. She was spoiling for a fight, only he wasn't ready to give her one. She dropped her eyes and tried to jerk out of his hold. 'Calm down,' he advised softly as he demonstrated how useless it was for her to struggle against his superior strength. This time, however, he was careful not to hurt her, using a minimal force to keep her there while some of the anger drained from her flushed cheeks. Then he said in a placating tone, 'I wanted to know if you intended to stick to our arrangement. I cannot watch you night and day when we get to the island, and your impulsiveness can be rather . . . alarming. I am sorry if my method was a little crude.'

'I suppose you think your trick worked,' she replied sullenly, reluctant to let go the last of her indignation, 'because I'm still here.'

He shrugged. 'Debatable, since it was so transparent to you.' His mouth quirked in an amused smile and he conceded, 'You're a bright girl, Alex Saunders.'

Not bright enough, Alex sighed exasperatedly as he put her firmly from him to strap up her packed suitcase. She didn't get him at all. Her latest display of temper seemed to have washed right over him—singularly appropriate, she judged, as a wayward humour conjured up the vision of him diving in search of his precious keys. She quelled it.

'Maybe you hoped I'd take off on my own?' she challenged as he lifted her suitcase off the bed. He gave her a bland look. It encouraged her to go further, relay her other nastier suspicion. 'Or was I to be arrested for car theft?'

He turned at the door, raising his eyebrows at her speculations. 'Believe it or not, neither thought had crossed my mind.'

'I bet!' It was sharp with disbelief.

'Otherwise,' the mocking smile spread across his handsome face, 'I just might not have disabled the car to make more noise than progress.'

There had been no risk of her getting away at all— how unfair! how devious! Alex fumed silently.

'How clever,' she murmured aloud, and took him back by returning his smile, suddenly viewing the whole episode with genuine amusement. 'But it's a shame you didn't seek my opinion of your scheme and save yourself so much trouble.'

Now his brows slanted quizzically. 'I know I shouldn't ask why.'

He didn't have to. Alex had every intention of telling him anyway. She moved towards him, her face alive with mischief as she opened the door and left him standing alone in the room to appreciate her smug parting shot of,

'I can't drive.'

The joke might finally have been on him, but his laughter reached her as she paused at the top of the stairs. It was a rich, pleasant sound. Bewildering man!

CHAPTER SEVEN

ANDROS saw she loved the boat ride. Her eyes were as bright as Nicky's, her laugh as exhilarated when he opened the throttle wide and the speedboat threw up spray in its path.

It was not a new experience for him; he had once made the journey regularly, would be making it often in the near future, yet he caught some of their enjoyment. He found himself prolonging it, making an unnecessarily wide sweep towards the island and obliquely studying the girl's profile. The wind was streaming the honey-gold hair back from her face and once more he thought her beautiful. He wished she wasn't.

She hated the house. He saw that too, as they stood viewing it from the end of the jetty.

'You don't like it?'

'It's very ...' Alex hesitated, then quickly offered, 'Imposing.'

'It was designed by a Swiss architect,' Andros qualified.

Was that good? All Alex knew was that she had never seen a house so large, so magnificently situated and so unremittingly ugly. It might positively breathe money, but style was something else. It didn't seem to have one—more like several, with its pillared entrance, Spanish archways and long french windows. To crown it all, it had a flat tiled roof.

'My father loved it,' he said with an unmistakable indulgence in his tone, and added, 'You do not look too pleased. I'd hoped its ... grandeur would compensate for the lack of entertainment on the island.'

It was a timely reminder to Alex that she was rudely gaping at his home. 'It's not that I don't find it beautiful,' she improvised hurriedly under his scrutiny.

'It's more that I'm not used to anywhere quite so big and . . .'

'And?' He lifted a quizzical brow.

'Well, it's different'—What was she saying?—'I mean interesting . . .' she said, floundering.

His laughter cut her short and he let her off the hook with a highly amused, 'I think the word you are searching for, Miss Saunders, is grotesque,' as he himself looked askance at the house above them.

Alex might have laughed herself if she hadn't been aware of who had her dangling on that hook in the first place. Not that her stony glance had much effect, especially when Nicky chose that moment to chime in, 'Why don't you call Lex Lex?'

'Why not?' Andros smiled at the boy's enquiry, apparently regarding it less awkward than it sounded. He directed at Alex, 'You mind?'

How could she? Without appearing ridiculous, although that about summed up their strange relationship.

'If you like.'

He nodded. 'I like,' he said, not quite matching her casualness. 'And you may call me Andros, yes?'

What a time to feel suddenly shy, acting like the teenager she wasn't far from being, Alex groaned as she avoided his gaze and mumbled, 'Yes, if you want.'

She sighed with relief when his attention was diverted by the burly middle-aged man in rough work clothes who descended the flight of steps from house to shoreline. Greeting him with a surprising warmth, Andros introduced the newcomer to Alex as Mario's stepfather, Spiro Kallides. She followed little of the man's guttural Greek, but answered his welcome with a friendly smile.

By the time she had run the gauntlet of the whole household, however, she had to force herself to keep smiling instead of following her inclination to snatch Nicky's hand, turn tail and run. She hadn't expected so many servants, such a difference from the simple way

Andros had lived on the mainland. She was totally
bemused by the sea of faces. Her nervousness was not
relieved by Andros at her side, relaxed in his attitude
towards his domestic staff and apparently oblivious of
the undercurrent of curiosity she could sense.

She wanted to ask how he intended to account for
Nicky and herself, but she decided to wait till they were
alone. He gave them a guided tour of room after room,
and if the house was a bit of a monstrosity—a rich
man's folly, Andros called it when they had paused in
the courtyard—the inside was, in contrast, tasteful and
elegant, upholstered in light shades of satin and
furnished mostly in sandalwood and pine and the finest
French cane. It was as large as many English country
houses but without any ponderous antiques that might
have made it a gloomy place. Although the rooms had
an unoccupied, lonely air about them now, it wasn't
difficult to imagine them filled with the love and
laughter of a family.

'My mother's province,' he explained, noting her
approval of the interior. 'She allowed my father to bully
the architect into building his "dream" house—a rather
disastrous hybrid of all the styles he admired—and then
she did her best to compensate.'

'It's very beautiful,' Alex confirmed as they climbed a
wide branching staircase to the upper floor.

The whole house was. The bedroom she had been
given was a luxury of soft cream carpeting, satin covers
and inlaid wardrobes fronted by gleaming mirrors.
Nicky's was perfect too for a little boy, and while she
settled him down for his afternoon nap she wondered
who had made the mobile of model aeroplanes that
hung from the roof or owned the football, boxing
gloves and other toys scattered on shelves and window
seats. Theo, she imagined, for she couldn't visualise his
older brother a child at all.

Later, when she wandered downstairs to the main
living room, she was forced to accept that he had been.
Among all the other family pictures that graced the

length of a sideboard, there he was—a solemn-faced child dressed in a sailor suit, his hair less wavy and with thinner features than the cherubic, grinning Theo—but surprisingly like a thoughtful Nicky: that must have been why she enjoyed looking at it, Alex told herself.

For when Kontos appeared at her shoulder to murmur, 'I think that is the first time you've smiled at me,' she clattered the gilt-edged frame back on its stand, her expression immediately losing any indulgence for him.

'Would you like a drink?' he asked before she could contradict him.

'A lime juice, please,' she agreed stiffly, and continued looking at the pictures.

'Here,' he handed her the glass and remained at her side. 'Does the boy like the room?'

'Yes, very much,' she admitted, and then for something to say, 'Was it yours or Theo's?'

'Theo's. We lived in Athens when I was a boy until my father made enough money to buy back the island.'

'Buy back?' she echoed.

'It belonged to my mother's family, but the original house was destroyed during the war, and the land was sold off afterwards.'

'By the Germans, I suppose,' Alex commiserated.

'No, actually the British bombed it,' he told her, and looked amused at her momentary discomfort. 'The Nazis had confiscated it and most of my grandfather's shipping line, and what was left by the end of the war, couldn't be salvaged. When my father married my mother against her family's wishes, he made up his mind to recover the island one day. Whether to please her or prove himself, I'm not sure.'

'Why didn't they approve of him?' Alex glanced at the picture of the elder Kontos. Unsmiling but as handsome as his first son, he had the same air of arrogance.

'Then he had little more than a half share in a small restaurant and some slightly bigger ideas,' he explained. 'You seem surprised?'

'Mario told me how big your hotel chain is,' she replied.

'What my father lacked in aesthetic taste, he made up for in business acumen,' he said, obviously admiring him for it. 'And he was a very determined man.'

'Or ruthless?' Alex dared to suggest.

'Perhaps,' he conceded with a wry smile, knowing she wasn't merely referring to his father's characteristics. 'When I returned from university, head full of ideas, he listened to the financial theories I had learned at Oxford, snorted with disgust and told me he'd found out more watching the black market operations after the war. I fell for it, of course, and spent the next decade trying to show him I was as good as he was.'

'And did you?' Alex asked, interested in spite of herself.

He shrugged. 'We moved into the rest of Europe at the beginning of the package holiday trade, and we were lucky—it boomed. My father intended to retire when Theo came into the business. Didn't *he* tell you anything about it?'

'Not much. He said his father owned a restaurant in Athens,' she recalled, undecided if it was curiosity or suspicion that prompted his question. Her gaze shifted to the studio photograph of her brother-in-law and she too was puzzled over why he had told Chris so little. Had he realised Chris would have been scared silly by wealth on this sort of scale?

'Maybe he wanted to be loved for himself,' Kontos speculated on a different train of thought.

'Maybe,' she answered shortly.

'And was he?' he returned—the first time he had shown any real interest in her feelings for his brother—but she heard the cynicism behind it. He watched her eyes move to the next photograph, one of Theo and a dark Greek girl in a casual embrace. 'Do you want to know who she was?'

She glanced back up at Andros and the baiting look in his eyes made her say, 'I think you're going to tell me anyway.'

'Her name's Helena,' he went on, 'a distant cousin—
and Theo's former fiancée.'

Was he trying to make her feel guilty? Alex wondered
as he delivered the information. Theo, of course, had
never mentioned any commitment back in Greece, but
she recalled how adamantly he had decried arranged
marriages. Now she guessed his feelings had applied to
his own situation.

'She's very pretty,' she offered, sensing that Kontos
expected a bitchier comment.

'But no competition to you, and you know it,' he said
accusingly.

'Do I?' she snapped back, not knowing *what* he
wanted her to say. She was sorry if the girl had cared
for Theo, but his deception couldn't have harmed her as
much as it had her own sister. 'It's obvious which of us
you'd have preferred as a sister-in-law.'

He didn't deny it. 'You wouldn't have been right for
Theo. He needed someone with a gentle nature.
Someone who would have made up for the strength he
lacked, simply by believing in him and being tolerant of
any shortcomings. Does that sound like you?'

'No,' she found herself admitting, startled by how
accurately he had described her sister Chris.

'And you certainly didn't need him.'

'So what do you think I need?' she said rashly,
irritated by his superior attitude. He didn't know *her*.

'A man you couldn't despise as weaker,' he said,
returning her angry stare measure for measure and
going further, 'who wouldn't put up with your
promiscuity and your careless insolence and your quick
temper . . . who'll slap you back the next time you raise
your hand to him,' he warned as he read the intention
in her eyes.

'A man such as yourself, I suppose,' Alex retorted.

'If you like,' he muttered, drawing so close he was all
but touching her and making her wish she had thought
twice about provoking him.

'No!' she denied hotly.

'No?' he challenged, almost as if he too felt the charge in the atmosphere that Alex couldn't quite translate as anger.

'No, I don't!' she exclaimed with a flare of that so ready temper which had her stamping from the room to hide the rising colour in her cheeks.

'Surplus to requirements'—that was how she later felt, as she sat in the splendid isolation of her bedroom, swinging a crossed leg back and forth to mark time. Nicky was off exploring with his uncle and she was too keyed up to sleep, even if her excuse of tiredness had been real.

She slipped off her sandals and curled her toes in the soft carpet, wondering where she went from here. She gazed at her clothes occupying the smallest corner of the wall-to-wall wardrobing and then at her reflection in its mirrors; it confirmed what she already knew. She was out of place amid such luxury. And she wasn't going to fit in—not in a million years, the mirror told her.

But Nicky was; for if her white jeans and plain cotton blouse had drawn some odd, covert glances, he had been taken at face value by the household. His dark colouring and features marked him a Kontos, and from the fond smiles of the female servants he was accepted as such, regardless of his sudden appearance.

And where did that leave her? The more Alex tried to look at the situation objectively, the more she saw it as impossible. She couldn't stay here indefinitely, not that Andros ever intended she should. Wherever that earlier conversation had been leading, it had scarcely been a speech of welcome. And for all her trying to convince herself otherwise, she minded very much what these people thought . . . what *he* thought.

If only she could work out a way of telling him the truth without her coming out of it as crazy or scheming—but she didn't have a great deal of confidence in Andros Kontos's capacity for mercy or understanding.

Yet as evening approached and she watched him climbing the rough steps from the shoreline, Nicky clinging to his back, she realised she might have to do it, sooner or later.

She lifted her hand, acknowledging Nicky's wave as he spotted her on the balcony. Tried to smile when he called up to her, 'You should have come, Lex!' but her lips were trembling as she fought back a drowning wave of sadness. She felt she was already losing him, even as he slipped his uncle's hold and came running into the house towards her.

She stared down at the man. He smiled up at her for a moment, almost as though he had forgotten who she was. She wished he hadn't. The plot was easier to follow when the baddie wore a black hat and a constant sneer—and didn't have a smile and the sort of compulsive looks that had begun to make *her* wonder how things would have been if they had met in other circumstances.

That had to be crazy! Alex decided as she caught the direction of her wandering imagination and turned back into the bedroom, abruptly breaking away from the man's gaze. She was grateful when Nicky burst into the room and didn't allow her to linger over the absurdity of herself and a Greek magnate having any common ground.

Alex drifted with the days. Three, four ... and then suddenly a fortnight had passed without her precisely losing the intention of telling Andros the truth, merely the willpower to do it.

It wasn't that she lacked opportunity. He might leave the house in the early morning, but he was always back by five, Nicky having quickly grown into the habit of sitting on the end of the jetty in the afternoon, waiting. Nervous of his falling into the sea, Alex kept him company until the speedboat appeared round the headland when she would withdraw into the house.

So yes, she had the chance, she supposed. In between dinner courses, if she could only overcome the ludicrousness she felt about holding a personal conversation across the twelve feet of table that separated them.

And she had got started once or twice, but his attitude hadn't been a great help. When she had dared to introduce Theo's name into the conversation, she had been coolly informed that he no longer wished to talk about her association with his brother.

Yet on neutral topics—world affairs, music, theatre, European history—discussion sometimes flowed with a natural, almost friendly, ease. He listened attentively to her views, often smiled at her humour, and if he made occasional dry witticisms to her wilder statements, they were probably justified.

But even while the situation between them improved, she sensed him biding his time, waiting for something. Some new development, she wasn't sure what, and her ideas on it tended to go in circles. If he wanted to find out more evidence to use against her for custody of Nicky, then why did he silence her the moment she as much as referred to Theo or Chris? Maybe he assumed she would lie . . . or maybe he had changed his mind and sent someone to London to conduct a thorough investigation into her background.

How many days, weeks would that take? Not many if he went straight to the social services. More, if his investigator tried to trace them back through all the short let flats they had had in two years.

She could be wrong. It wasn't as though he behaved guiltily when she caught him watching her across that great expanse of table; he even had the nerve to smile at her. But if she were correct, wasn't it one more reason to volunteer the information first and hope 'coming clean' would weigh in her favour.

For now she knew when she left, it would be on her own. Her love for Nicky had not diminished. The strength of his affection didn't weaken as he grew fond of his uncle. It had been foolish of her to be scared that it would. But on the island, with all the time in the world to think, she could more clearly separate love and need.

Nicky didn't have to ask, 'We're not going back to London, are we, Lex?' for her to know she shouldn't . . . couldn't ever take him away from Greece now. She watched him blossom in the Mediterranean sun, lose that sickly pallor, run wild with Mario's eight-year-old half-brother, Dimitri, over land that might one day be his. He needed this life, not a tiny flat in a city back street.

And herself? She didn't belong here. She had to tell the truth and hope that Andros had pity enough to allow her contact with Nicky as he grew up, understanding for why she had deceived him in the first place. Soon.

As he sat in Stephanos's plush office, pity was the farthest emotion from what Andros Kontos felt on his initial hurried scanning of the report. Blind fury would have been closer to the mark. Nor did it figure largely when he went over it a second time and tried to make sense of what the girl had allowed him to believe in the light of the details it disclosed.

'Well?' Stephanos prompted when his friend still hadn't said anything.

He got more reaction than he'd bargained for in, 'The lying, deceiving, little bitch!'

'I'm not sure I like the way you're smiling, Ros,' he murmured, an understatement as he read things into Andros's expression. 'Let's leave it to a court, yes?'

'No, I don't think so,' Andros replied, his concentration only partly on what the lawyer was saying.

Stephanos sensed his abstraction. More forcefully he added, 'Look, Ros, we'll get custody without a shadow of a doubt. Just be grateful it's not going to be as messy as we supposed.'

'I don't feel grateful,' Andros drawled back.

'That's what I'm afraid of,' the other man grimaced. Andros was usually the most rational of men, but right at the moment he wasn't sure what was going on in his friend's mind. 'If you don't want to go to court, Ros, show her the report and make her realise that with what you can offer, given your equal relationship to the child she doesn't stand a chance against you.'

'And then?' Andros allowed his friend to feel he was earning his fee.

'I know you won't like it,' Stephanos held his hands up, a plea to be heard out; 'but if she was after higher stakes, it might be easier if you still buy her off—a vastly reduced sum, of course.'

Slowly Andros shook his head, saying, 'I don't think that is a good idea. Alex Saunders has a very careless way with bank drafts.'

Stephanos was lost as to what that meant or the smile that had returned to Andros's face. 'No court battle, no pay-off—so what else can you do?' he pointed out their limited choices.

'I'll think of something,' Andros murmured drily, and rose to conclude the meeting with a firm handshake.

'I don't like the sound of that,' Stephanos replied, only half joking and unreassured by the bland look he received in return. He made a last effort, voicing a suspicion, 'You've said the girl's very sharp. For all the fact that she's a lot younger than you imagined and perhaps less experienced—we couldn't find out much on that angle—Ros, has it occurred to you that she might be out to land herself a rich Greek husband?'

When Andros's rich deep laughter eventually quietened to a smile of pure amusement, Stephanos was left alone, shaking his head over the whole business.

What was he *playing* at?

'I *repeat*, "Good evening",' penetrated Alex's self-absorption across the dining room table when Andros was obliged to pitch his voice higher.

'Sorry.' She jerked her head up to catch his tolerant expression for her abstraction, and felt an immediate blush hit her cheeks. Her stilted, 'Good evening,' was

directed at the table and became the first words they
had exchanged since his return from Athens.

'Did you have a pleasant day?' Andros asked with his
usual politeness that had ceased to irritate when she
realised it was ingrained, not forced.

'Yes, fine,' Alex mumbled automatically, and
conceded wryly to herself that yes, apart from drifting
through yet another day wondering how long it would
last or what she had done about explaining their
relationship to the other occupants of the island or
whether he had discovered the truth about her . . .

'You don't like oysters?' Andros's deep tones once
more interrupted her erratic musings.

'No, they're fine,' Alex assured him, and only realised
why he had asked when she noticed rather than stared
rigidly at her untouched plate. In her hurry to cover up
the silliness of her answer, she sent her fork clattering to
the floor.

'Leave it,' she was ordered, an impatience creeping
into his voice as she bent to retrieve it. Nevertheless it
was muted in his, 'What's wrong, Alex?'

'Wrong?' she echoed, making herself look at him.
Why couldn't he have been in one of his broodingly
silent moods? 'No, everything's just . . .'

'I know—fine,' he finished for her with a mildly
sarcastic inflection.

Damn it, couldn't he respect her need for silence once
in a while? She did his, no matter how much she
loathed the heavy atmosphere it created.

'Yes,' she snapped with finality, and dropped her eyes
pointedly back to her meal.

It did not discourage him. 'You are very quiet,' he
said, then paused for comment. When none was
forthcoming he continued musingly, 'Believe it or not, I
find myself missing your chatter.'

'I do not *chatter*!' Alex rose unthinkingly to the bait.

'Talk, then,' he suggested blandly. 'My English, it is
not always good,' he added for good measure, suddenly
acquiring a heavier accent.

His English, it was aggravatingly near perfect, Alex condemned, stiffening against that surprisingly teasing manner he had developed towards her.

'If you must know ...' she hesitated, desperately searching for a good reason for her silence, 'conducting conversations at long-range distance inhibits my inclination to ... *chatter!*'

'Yes, I take your point,' he responded in dry agreement, and Alex bent her head back to her meal with a sigh of relief.

'What are you doing!' she exclaimed, more startled by the suddenness with which he had appeared at her side than angry when he lifted her plate and wine glass.

'What does it look like I am doing?' was the amused reply as he set them down in front of the chair next to his. 'You can manage the cutlery, can't you?' he prompted while Alex still sat gaping at the other end of the table.

'I didn't mean ...' she trailed off, calling herself all kinds of idiot for the remark that had got her into this. Either she could remain stubbornly seated where she was and end up looking foolish by making an issue over what his tone plainly suggested was nothing—or she could move.

She moved.

Andros tucked her chair in behind her, and resumed his seat. 'Better?' he enquired with another of his bland smiles.

Worse, much worse, Alex groaned to herself, but in the face of his suave good humour, she managed, 'Yes, it's fi ... easier.'

'A table like this,' he gestured at its size, 'is intended for a large family. As you say, for two people it is a trifle absurd. I myself would have suggested this seating arrangement earlier, but ...' he shrugged.

Was that light mockery in his voice? Of course it was, Alex decided. Her body tensed at his proximity as he filled up her wine glass.

'I hope you do not feel this inhibiting too,' he

remarked smoothly after seconds had ticked by without any response from her.

Impulsively she spoke her thoughts aloud. 'Won't the servants think it strange?'

'Think *what* strange?' A frown creased his forehead at her enquiry.

'I mean,' she tried to rescue it, 'my moving, us sitting together . . .'

'Why?' he asked when Alex stammered to a halt.

'They might get the wrong idea,' she said, sounding vague and silly even to her own ears.

'From us sitting together?' he repeated, slanting her a look that told her she was being slightly absurd. 'Which wrong idea would that be, Alex?'

He could afford to find it amusing as he waited for her answer, but Alex was wishing she hadn't said anything at all.

'I don't know. It doesn't matter,' she said with her usual evasion, bowing her head again and thus starting when his fingers suddenly touched her hand.

'Calm down,' he advised as he resisted her immediate attempt to slip his hold.

'I am perfectly calm,' she retorted.

'Really?' His thumb brushed the pulse at her wrist, leaping more frantically than ever at his gentle touch. 'Something seems to have upset you, Alex. I demand . . .' he paused, grimacing as his natural arrogance asserted itself and covering her hand with his, went on, '. . . I would like to know what.'

Why tonight of all nights? she moaned inwardly, did he have to make it so difficult for her to hide behind her flippancy?

'I want to tell you, that is, I need to say,' she began clumsily, 'I need to . . . Oh, Lucia!' she exclaimed at the sudden appearance of the cook-housekeeper behind his highbacked chair.

'I'm sorry,' she mumbled with acute embarrassment as she knocked over her glass by urgently jerking her hand from underneath his. The dark red wine spilled in a dramatic stain over the white linen. 'I'm awfully sorry,' she repeated in Italian to Lucia, Mario's mother, who reacted more quickly, mopping up the surplus with a napkin before it could drip on to Alex's lap.

The dark buxom woman smiled, reassuring a flustered Alex that the mark would not be permanent and producing a smaller square of cloth to hide the damage. There was something almost motherly in her tone that made Alex react even more like a gauche child, utterly conscious of Andros's growing exasperation.

'Very well, what is going on around here?' he said impatiently once they were alone again.

'Alex?'

The change in his tone was marked. If she had had any chance to confess in stark, impersonal tones, she seemed to have lost it.

And the nerve to do so, for she murmured, 'Nothing is going on.'

'You knock over your wine glass . . .'

'I've apologised, haven't I?'

'. . . Act as though you've just committed a crime,' he overrode her terse interruption, 'and then Lucia gives me a look that suggests I should be punished for it. But nothing's going on . . .? What tales have you been telling behind my back?'

'None!' This time her reply was forceful. 'It isn't *my place* to tell your servants anything.'

'Meaning?' he shot back with all that cold aggression that had typified their early encounters. Fool that she had been to imagine things had changed; his distrust of her was as strong as ever.

'Oh, work it out for yourself!' she flared, pushing back her chair.

'Sit down!' he barked.

'You're hurting me,' she protested through gritted teeth as her wrist twisted in his bruising grip.

'Then sit down,' he repeated, but didn't give her time to comply, using his strength to jerk her back in her seat.

Alex's face was a study of pride and resentment as their eyes clashed. Very slowly he released her hand and waited till it was clear she wasn't going to make another move before saying, 'And what do you feel *I* should have told my household staff?'

Did he have to sound so condescending? Alex fumed. 'The truth,' she replied rashly.

He slanted her a dry look. 'I would have thought the facts speak for themselves, Alex. Nicky is very like a Kontos. I am sure the servants see the similarity. You are Nicky's mother. Is there anything more you would like to add?' he queried, his eyebrows raising quizzically.

For a long moment, looking into those piercing eyes holding hers, she imagined them actually willing her to answer, to treat the question seriously. But while she searched for the words to tell him the full truth, she saw in their depths the cynicism that had forced her initial deviation from it.

She looked away. 'Right plot but wrong hero, perhaps,' she finally stated, silently adding 'And wrong heroine too' as she lacked the courage to do so out loud.

'I see,' was his only comment after he had time to absorb her cryptic remark.

Alex doubted it very much. 'They might think that you and I . . . that we're . . . that . . .' she heard her own incoherence as she struggled to overcome her reluctance to voice her concern. But if it seemed absurd to her that people would link her and Andros, there was something in Lucia's attitude which made her go on, '. . . That *you're* Nicky's father,' and then wait his reaction.

She waited so long, at first she questioned if she had heard *him* properly when he eventually did speak.

'You didn't *consider* that?' she echoed incredulously as he raised his wine glass to his lips. 'Is that *all* you're going to say?'

'What do you want me to say?' he asked, turning his head to appraise her flushed features.

'I don't think you understand.' She surely hadn't got through. 'I think they might believe that you and I . . .'

'Were lovers,' he supplied bluntly at her faltering, and with a sarcastic edge, added, 'Despite your painful attempt to avoid specifics, I can move backwards from Nicky's birth to the act of conception.'

'And forwards?' she demanded.

'Are lovers, then,' he astounded her with his bland correction.

Alex shook her head to clear it. 'Aren't you going to do anything?'

'Do what?' It sounded remarkably like a challenge.

'I don't know!' she exclaimed in frustration. More than sit there, coolly sipping his wine. 'Doesn't it bother you?' she cried in disbelief. Hadn't he sensed Lucia's disapproval?

'Less than it appears to bother you, Alex,' he said, leaning back in his chair to view her with a dispassionate interest. 'I am not ashamed of Nicky being thought my son . . . are you?'

'Am I what?' He was confusing her totally with his attitude.

'Ashamed of Nicky being . . . your son?' he jibed.

God, what a mess she'd got herself into!

'That's not the point,' she appealed for him to see what was, having given up the idea of telling him anything more radical.

He did. 'So the servants, they might think we are lovers,' he said with a shrug. His smile was sardonic as his eyes travelled slowly over the top half of her figure and back to her face. 'Despite the clothes, I don't think my taste would be faulted that much.'

Was he *trying* to be infuriating? Or did he just not give a damn about other people's opinions?

'You may not care,' she snapped furiously, 'but the idea of you and me, I find . . . humiliating!'

'So I've gathered,' he returned, all signs of amusement disappearing from his handsome face to leave an emotionless mask.

She tried again. 'You've *got* to tell them they've got it wrong!'

His eyes narrowed at her commanding tone. '*I* don't *have* to do anything,' he stressed with a harsh arrogance, and then, his mouth curving with contempt, he went on, 'And as for defending your virtue, Miss Saunders, are you sure it isn't a bit too late for that?'

At the end of her tether, Alex caught him completely off guard with her sudden exit. Half colliding with Lucia in the doorway, she mumbled a hasty apology and left Andros, now out of his chair and in the middle of yelling an order for her to come back, to explain away her behaviour.

She took the cliff steps down to the beach below, almost falling in her haste to be clear of the house. No truth in his taunt, she didn't know why she let it upset her. But it did.

When she reached the sand, she didn't stop but ran along the edge of the water, careless of the soaking her trouser legs were getting. She filled her confused head with the clear sounds of the sea and the night. It was growing dark, but she ran until she was breathless and exhausted. Collapsing on to the sand, she hugged her knees to her chin and watched the advancing and receding of the sea till it hypnotised her into a state beyond thought or feeling.

Only it couldn't last—just as she couldn't escape Andros merely by running from his house. She saw him a long way off, strolling along the shoreline now bathed in moonlight and following her footprints in the sand till he stood within a few yards of her.

'Why did you run?' he asked outright when she did not acknowledge him. Alex hunched her shoulders and was startled by his quietly-spoken question of, 'Are you crying, Alex?'

'No . . . of course not,' she denied, after she brushed the back of her hand hastily across her damp cheeks, and lifted her head to prove it. 'I just wanted to be alone for a while,' she mumbled, rising to her feet.

As if ignoring her reply, Kontos remained motionless beside her, neither approaching closer nor moving off.

Each turned to face the sea outlined so clearly by the bright moonlight, and for once the silence between them was not oppressive.

The waves washed over the fine sand with a rhythmic motion, the pattern of sound repeating itself over and over. Alex could feel herself being held by its magic—quivering slightly at the spell cast by moon and darkness.

Andros had slipped off his jacket and wrapped it around her thin, short-sleeved blouse before she could object. It was warm from his body, but she shivered again as the silk lining touched her skin. Gently he took her hand, and making no justification for the action, led her back along the beach.

They retraced their steps without speaking until they were within sight of the house. Turning towards her, Andros pulled the jacket lapels together, protectively, and said softly, 'If it's important to you, Alex, I'll ensure the servants know we are not lovers.'

'I don't understand,' she whispered, as much to herself as to him. She hadn't tried to wrest her hand out of the engulfing warmth of his, hadn't wished for an end to their slow, silent stroll along the moonlit beach.

'I wanted to hurt you,' he murmured under his breath, and his hands slid beneath the jacket to mould the delicate bones of her shoulders.

'Don't . . .' Alex's protest was dangerously weak and breathless.

It was ignored as warm persuasive fingers slipped inside the neckline of her blouse to spread against the base of her slender throat.

'But not any more,' he continued, unnecessarily for what Alex recognised in the dark eyes holding hers was far from a promise of cruelty. Her small desperate grip on his arm did not remove his hand but momentarily stilled any further attempt at intimacy as he asked, 'Do you really find it so humiliating? . . . To be thought my woman?'

She should have, if only for the way he phrased it—

as though it would make her a possession. Instead, a strange unbidden excitement stirred her senses to wonder what it would be like. She should break free, but she felt no surprise or anger when the hand on her shoulder tightened at her attempt to do so.

'See it my way,' she appealed. 'You're rich and highly eligible on most counts. Whereas I'm so clearly out of your class that I must seem like a cheap gold-digger or an odd amusement on your part.'

She saw he was on the point of interrupting and she rushed on, 'That's what I find degrading. I didn't mean anything personal to you.'

'I'm glad to hear it,' he replied with a deceptively amused smile.

'Then let me go?' She strove to sound casual.

'Not yet,' he murmured. 'I'm not hurting you now, am I, Alex?'

He knew he wasn't! The fingers that had shifted to her neck were moving in a slow insinuating caress that made the breath catch in her throat.

'Please, Andros!'

'Please what, Alex?' It was the softest of taunts that mocked the breathlessness his sure, knowing touch was arousing, but it was enough to spark Alex's own pride.

'Stop playing with me!' she cried aloud, at last wresting out of his grasp. Perhaps she wouldn't have run if he hadn't immediately reached out for her, but run she did, wild and blind, away from the house, vainly clutching at the hope he wouldn't pursue.

She made at most ten yards and had a split second warning before she found herself falling on to the fine sand and rolled over to stare up at the face of her captor. His hands were no longer gentle as they restrained her from hitting out at him, and pushed her back down on to the soft bed of sand. She tried to use her legs, but his body was hard with bone and muscle and easily trapped her slim frame with its weight. He held her arms above her head, but still she struggled, twisting and writhing her body in anger against his domination until she finally exhausted herself.

Only then did he ease off her slightly, waiting for her breathing to level out as her breasts heaved. And watched as the fight went out of her eyes and her fear grew.

He caught her chin when she would have turned her head away. 'And if I'm not *playing*?' he muttered, compelling her to acknowledge the desire that darkened his eyes with the pain and pleasure of it.

Without experience Alex could still recognise the fevered excitement her struggling had aroused, but she knew too little of her own body to understand why her fear should suddenly turn to something sweet and fierce and clamouring that willed her to respond to it.

As his head lowered slowly towards hers and she tasted the cool breath on the warm male lips which covered her own, any last dying voice of reason gave way. His first explorative kiss sought to give rather than take pleasure before brushing over her cheek to trail softly against her neck. And when he moved back from her on to his side and released her arms to pull her body gently nearer him, she could no longer remember why she needed to fight him. He didn't want to hurt her; he'd said so. He just wanted to . . .

The thought was lost as his hand pushed forward to cup the soft rounded flesh of one breast and then, in a slow tantalising movement, stroke its peak, instantly hardening with arousal. A low moan of desire escaped Alex's parted lips as she gave up thinking at all to twine her fingers in his crisp dark hair.

At first, the feeling was all pleasure, unfamiliar in its drugging sweetness as his lips followed the trail of his fingers, and then became longing as he began to suck and tease her flesh till her hands clasped round his neck, her body arching instinctively in an unconscious invitation.

In one fluid movement, he pushed her down on her back before his head swooped down to kiss her again, his lips now hard and demanding, exploring her mouth with an intimacy for which she was unprepared. Excitement became panic in one shattering moment.

He might have been forgiven misinterpreting the nails suddenly digging into his back for the passion that had been as fresh and stimulating as the girl's fury but when his hand slid over the flat of her stomach and then urgently tugged at the thin belt looped in her jeans, there was no mistaking her cry of total rejection as her mouth managed to escape his.

But he continued his lovemaking, now whispering hoarse words of persuasion in his own, more familiar language. Words meaningless to a young English girl trembling with fright in his arms.

He had every reason to believe she had led him to this point with full knowledge of what she was doing and in shame at her abandoned response to his skilful loving, she almost saw he had the right to take her regardless of her protests.

Indeed when he raised his head to become aware of the tears coursing down her soft skin, it was to demand in angry frustration, 'Say you want me, Alex. Damn you, say it!' as his body ground down on hers to make her feel how much he wanted her.

She said nothing. There was nothing to say. She had wanted him. An insistent ache suggested she still did. But the silent plea in her panicked eyes conveyed more feeling than even Alex realised. She couldn't quite believe it when Andros rolled away from her and levered himself to his feet to face the sea.

She was still staring at him when he turned back to her and muttered angrily, 'For pity's sake, Alex, dress yourself!' His eyes raked the full, beautiful breasts still exposed to his view.

Wide-eyed and dumb with shock, she flew to button the front of her blouse with clumsy, fumbling fingers. Then, her sense of humiliation unbearable, she began to cry in earnest—great sobs that racked her shaking body—and she recoiled at his appoach.

Only her fear was unwarranted, for he simply draped his discarded jacket round her heaving shoulders and backed away from her again.

'Stop crying, Alex!' he ordered, and succeeded in making her cry all the harder. It made him feel inadequate and as guilty as if he had actually raped her and not just considered it for that one mad moment.

It had all gone wrong, somehow! And the only thing he was certain of was that those tears had been real enough. Sensing she wished him gone, he silently retraced his steps to the house.

In the darkness of the wide pillared porchway, he waited for what seemed an eternity until slow steps translated themselves into the half-crouching figure of the girl.

She passed so close to him that for an instant he could not believe she had not seen him. The moonlight reflecting in those tear-washed eyes showed an anguish and turmoil that seemed accusing—and then she was gone from him, disappearing into the darkness of the hallway.

Once more he damned her, but now there was despair in the curse.

CHAPTER EIGHT

SOME sixth sense told Andros not to leave for work the next morning.

From his balcony, he saw her leaving the house by a side entrance and fought the impulse to follow her down the cliff steps to the jetty below. For even if the boy hadn't been with her, what could he say? That he was sorry for whatever had made her cry?—when a part of him was actually more sorry now that he hadn't ignored her tears and made her want him as much as he did her. That he wouldn't try to make love to her?—when he knew he would make it a lie if he ever sensed her open and vulnerable to him again.

So he stayed where he was and watched—for what he wasn't sure. They reached the end of the duckboards and the boy jumped into one of the moored speedboats while she sat at the edge of the jetty, looking out to sea. Imagining herself somewhere else? he wondered, but with no real awareness of how close he was to her thinking.

Half an hour passed until Nicky tired of playing with the boat's instrumentation and the pretence of steering its streamlined shape through the water and clambered back out on to the jetty. Alex must have called to him because he checked his run towards the house and came back to where she was sitting. She pulled the boy down beside her and half-turned so she was facing him. From her profile she seemed to be talking earnestly to the child, whose responses appeared briefer and briefer until they were confined to that grave nod of intelligence which had made Andros himself smile often enough.

But he was frowning now as his eyes followed the small figure that walked back along the pier, dejectedly mounted the cliff steps and then broke into a run the moment he reached the courtyard. By the time Andros intercepted his flight at the top of the wide staircase, the tears were streaming down Nicky's pain-stricken face.

Having carried the boy to his bedroom, Andros sent the maid who had come to investigate the noise to fetch Lucia, and went through to the adjoining bathroom to rifle the medicine cabinet for the inhaler he felt might be needed.

When he crossed back to the bed, however, Nicky's crying had tailed off to a pitiful whimper, his misery turned into the pillow he was clutching fiercely.

'Come, Nicky, what is wrong?' Andros urged softly.

The boy resisted his gentle effort to turn him on his back, so his reply was muffled. But Andros caught one word at least—'leaving'. He gathered the boy up by his arms to face him.

'Listen to me, Nicky—whatever it is, I'll fix it.'

Nicky stared up at his uncle, wanting to believe the absolute conviction he saw in the man's eyes but fighting back another sob to say, 'Can't . . .'

'I'll fix it,' Andros repeated with hard determination. 'Just tell me what she said.'

It dried the boy's tears but he wavered, 'Mustn't tell before . . .'

Andros had no difficulty working out whose instruction that was. Suppressing anger, he prompted firmly, 'You don't want to leave, do you, Nicky?'

Nicky's face was a mass of uncertainty. 'No, but if Lex isn't going to stay . . .' he faltered. 'Lex says . . .'

'What does Lex say, Nicky?' Andros encouraged with a deceptive mildness, and when the boy still looked doubtful, he lied unashamedly, 'I won't let her know you told me. Trust me.'

Nicky wanted to, because he had grown fond of his tall dark uncle even if he was sometimes very stern. But he loved Alex more, and confused as he felt, he intuitively understood that to please one was not necessarily to please the other. In the end, with a child's self-centredness, he chose to please himself.

'She says she can't stay. She's got to go back to London. She doesn't like it here,' Nicky revealed in jerky tones, the last his own interpretation of the situation and the rest a much abridged version of the careful way Alex had explained her plans. 'Make her like it, Uncle Ros,' he added, eyes enormous with pleading.

'I see,' Andros said curtly, exerting a tight control over his mounting fury with the girl.

Like his aunt the night before, Nicky found it a highly unsatisfactory answer. He tugged at his uncle's sleeve and demanded, 'You'll make it all right?'

Andros nodded. 'I'll make it all right,' he promised with the firm intention of doing so; if Alex Saunders thought he was about to let her and the boy return to England, she was going to be thoroughly disillusioned.

When the Italian housekeeper appeared in the doorway he detached the boy's arms from around his neck and tipped his chin to look at him again.

'No more crying now?'

'No,' Nicky agreed solemnly, and worried over his uncle's opinion, added, 'I hardly ever cry, Uncle Ros. You can ask Lex.'

Andros forced a smile and ruffled the boy's hair before asking Lucia to keep an eye on him for a little while, explaining the use of the plastic inhaler if it should prove necessary. Then he went in search of Alex.

He tracked her down to the lounge, sitting curled up in the corner of the sofa, and he announced his presence by letting the door slam behind him. The sudden noise had her head jerking up. She looked totally disconcerted to see him standing there.

Her eyes skirted away from his, but her recovery was slow as she stammered, 'I . . . I didn't expect you to be home.'

'I'm sure you didn't,' he responded on a harsh note of anger.

If she heard it, she found the nerve to shrug, 'You're usually at work by this time, that's all.' She uncoiled her legs and made to rise, but he was quicker.

'Where do you think you are going?' he rapped out. Her mouth set insolently as she looked up at him, towering above her, but at least she thought better of moving.

'I wanted to check on Nicky,' she muttered in reply.

'He's in his room. I've just been talking to him,' he said with heavy significance.

'Oh!' Her eyes lowered to her lap.

He waited for her to make some other comment but grew annoyed with her silence and himself for even giving her the chance to improve the look of things.

'And when were you considering leaving?' he bit out, in an unmistakable sarcasm.

He had not anticipated a direct answer, far less one with a total absence of guilt as she murmured quietly, 'Tomorrow, I suppose. I *was* going to tell you.'

'Tomorrow!' he repeated explosively, and yanked her to her feet to demand, 'What damn game are you playing now, Alex Saunders?'

'No game!' She tried to twist out of his bruising grip, and came back flippantly, 'I'm leaving—but don't bother reaching for your cheque book, my air ticket will do.'

'Like hell you are!' he shouted back, shaking her for the bold defiance that flashed in her eyes. 'You're mad if you think I'd let you leave Greece now with that boy . . .'

'I'm not . . .' Alex tried to interrupt, but he overrode her objection.

'Whatever selfish reasons you have for rejecting what I'm offering, Nicky wants to stay here with me. Understand?'

'Of course I do. I can see how much Nicky loves it here, that's why . . .'

'You know!' He stared at her with a mixture of contempt and disbelief. 'And you'd still take him back to the sort of life you had in London? You make me . . .'

'I can guess,' Alex cut in angrily—she'd had enough.

'If you'll *just listen!* I asked Nicky to let me tell you, but
. . . Anyway, you must have misunderstood him. *I'm*
leaving. *He's not.* Understand?' she finished in a tone of
anger and exasperation.

For a full minute Andros was stunned into silence
while he struggled to appreciate what she was saying.

'You're leaving the boy behind?' She nodded, but he
relied on his own instincts and rejected it with, 'I don't
believe you.'

A thin smile mocked his suspicion. 'Wait and see,
then.' She sounded almost careless about it, but her
direct gaze told him she was serious before it slid
pointedly to the hands gripping her arms. 'For now,
you can dispense with the *brute* force, or I might think
you *want* me to stay!'

Rage welled within him as he tightened his pressure—
but only succeeded in feeling worse when the girl bit on
her bottom lip against the pain he was inflicting. With a
smothered curse, he sent her from him.

He took several steadying breaths before he followed
her to the window. She was staring out at the sea again,
perhaps already far from Greece in her mind. He found
he couldn't come to terms with that thought very easily.

But rather than give up the offensive, he rasped, 'And
what about the boy? You're just going to walk out on
him. Was that an act too—all that loving affection you
give him?'

Her mouth tightened. 'Nicky knows how I feel.'

'Does he?' he bit out. 'Well, I'm damned if I do!'

'*You* don't have to,' she replied stonily, but when he
failed to respond and instead began to study her profile,
she added less confidently, 'And I've explained it to
Nicky. He wants to stay, but I can't. He understands.'

'Not well enough, apparently,' Andros muttered with
a heavy irony that earned him a sideways glance. He
pressed on, 'Oh, he told me you don't like it here, but
only after he stopped sobbing his heart out over your
leaving.'

Now he had all her attention. 'Is he all right?'

'Do you care?' he flipped back, knowing his accusation unfair.

'Damn you, Andros Kontos, you're getting what you want!' she cried back, wheeling round to confront him. 'Do you have to make it difficult for me just because I wouldn't . . .' she broke off.

'What I want? And how would you know what I want?' His eyes lowered to the swell of her breasts but moved quickly back to the level of her forehead as if he was forcing himself away from the incidents of the previous night.

Sensing his indecision, Alex made to escape, but he quickly blocked her path.

'No, Miss Saunders, you're not running out on this. I have a small nephew upstairs to whom you owe an explanation and who seems to love you.'

Before she could adapt to his latest change of mood, Alex found herself being half pushed, half dragged up the stairs and along the corridor to Nicky's room.

He forced her inside the door and gestured silently for the housekeeper to leave them alone.

The sight of Nicky lying on the bed, clutching his teddy bear, brought a lump to Alex's throat. She had thought she had explained it so well down on the jetty. He hadn't said much, but he seemed to have understood that she wasn't abandoning him in any unloving way, merely leaving him with his uncle instead of his father. But now she saw from his pale tear-stained face that he had been holding in his feelings, pretending to please her.

When he looked up and called her name on a high broken note, she acted instinctively. He was in her arms before she had sunk down on the bed. Head buried in her neck and his body, so small and thin, clinging to hers, he began to cry again, low and whimpering.

'Oh, Nicky, you mustn't cry,' she begged, but her own voice was thick with held-back tears.

'Don't leave me, Lex!' he said on a sob. 'You promised you'd never leave me.'

'I know, Nick, I know,' she soothed, while she searched for words to explain why she was forced to go back on that vow, all too conscious of the man listening as well. Quietly she murmured, 'But I'm not really leaving you. I've got to go back to London for a little while, that's all. And you know you like it here, so it's better if you stay with Uncle Ros. Do you see, Nicky?'

It didn't receive a direct reply, more a loud wail of protest that had her unconsciously raising her eyes to Andros.

'Help me,' she mouthed.

He shook his head. 'I'm sorry, Alex, but like Nicky I don't see why you're doing this.'

'You know I can't stay,' she pleaded for him at least to admit openly there could be no place for her here.

'Do I?' It was the softest of challenges and strangely the feeling that flowed between them, changing and indefinable, did not touch on anger. 'What if I asked you to?'

He was still holding her eyes when Nicky began to choke on his tears, and this time he answered the mute appeal in her gaze.

Very gently he took the child from her and wiped his tears, but his voice and his expression were firm as he instructed, 'Stop crying now, Nicky. I told you I'd make it right, didn't I?'

'Yes,' Nicky gulped, and his tears were largely stemmed as he waited for his uncle to perform the miracle.

'You would prefer to go back to London with your . . . mother rather than stay here without her, wouldn't you?' his uncle quizzed, and Nicky's tremulous nod and Alex's protest were simultaneous.

'What are you doing?' she gasped in horror.

She was answered obliquely as Andros went on in the same sure, heavy tone, 'So we'll leave the choice up to her, yes?'

'Yes, all right.' Nicky matched his uncle's sober manner. And two pairs of eyes turned towards her expectantly—Nicky with his wide eyes pleading with her to change her mind about leaving Greece, and Andros—could she almost believe he felt the same way? No, it must be a trick of the light, or maybe a trick of a different sort, like last night.

But already she could see he had won this new game. She couldn't have taken Nicky away from here, even if she had the option, and she was almost certain she hadn't—this charade was for Nicky's benefit, a calculated risk on *his* part. But she couldn't reject Nicky outright. She would have to stay while he felt he needed her: it would take time—perhaps until he started school and would not notice her absence so keenly.

And what about herself? For seconds she dwelled on thoughts and fears that milled through her head and then forcibly clamped down on them as they threatened to overwhelm her.

Surely she could ignore the emotions of last night?— they weren't real—she couldn't be attracted to *him*. It was simply the setting, the full golden moon and the sea washing on the breathlessly silent seashore, as trite as the imagery of love songs and romantic novels. It was some strange sick curiosity that had allowed his hands and mouth to give her that first experience of the power of a man's lovemaking. It was—anything but *him*. And she wouldn't ever let it happen again.

'Very well, Nicky, I'll stay . . . for a little while longer, but . . .' the rest was choked off by one of his tight hugs but as she met Andros's eyes over the little boy's shoulder, she added for the man alone. 'You shouldn't have done that. I have to talk to you.'

'Later.' He broke off his deep, fathomless stare and was gone, leaving Alex determined to make it soon.

As the day wore on with Nicky her constant shadow and Andros, still on the island but conducting his business on the telephone in the privacy of his study, Alex assumed he meant later to be at dinner after Nicky was in bed.

Yet for all her anxiety to straighten out the whole muddled situation, a bout of nerves gripped her minutes before the meal and robbed her of the rehearsed speech she had prepared. It should have relieved her, but she felt resentment mingled with embarrassment when she walked in on the maidservant in the middle of re-setting the table. Based on the previous evening, the Greek girl had obviously used her initiative in laying the table only to receive countermanding instructions from Andros already seated at its head. Alex had a childish urge to do an about-turn and show him she didn't even want to sit in the same room as him and eat his food.

But he had risen at her entrance and was now holding out her usual chair for her. Earlier he had been casual in slacks and a fine wool sweater, but he had changed for dinner into one of his dark, superbly-tailored suits. She had always been aware on one level of his forbiddingly handsome looks, but now she seemed to have lost any defence against their physical impact as her heart skipped a beat and then another as he returned her interest with a curiously intent look.

Her eyes skittered away from him and she moved quickly to her place, cross with herself for feeling a sudden dissatisfaction with her own less than elegant appearance. She mumbled a reply to his stiffly formal greeting, but her resolve to set the pace of the conversation began to weaken when he made no effort to follow it up after the first course was served and they were alone.

Determinedly she raised her head to say something, but the words lodged in her throat when her gaze levelled with his. It wasn't that she didn't have his attention, quite the reverse, as she discovered herself the subject of his steady, measured appraisal.

Typically he evinced no embarrassment at being caught staring, but while Alex tried to appear unabashed she felt the memory of last night as an almost tangible force between them and, unnerved by it, she lowered her eyes back to the table. They were fixed on it for the rest of the meal, and unlike the last they had shared he didn't attempt to invade the privacy of her thoughts.

Unfortunately he didn't have to. He was the central overshadowing image in the confusion that had made her see leaving as imperative from the second she had woken that morning from a restless sleep. Acting on instincts of self-preservation, she had honestly believed Nicky was ready to cope without her. And still, when her own heart was breaking at his tearful pleading, she would have had the strength to leave him, knowing he would ultimately have to adjust to the separation.

But Andros had made it impossible for her with his intervention. She blamed herself for being stupid enough to turn to him for help in handling Nicky, expecting him to support her decision, despite his anger downstairs. *That* she had put down to a reaction against her making her own plans, even after he realised Nicky wasn't included in them. So she was not prepared for the way he had manipulated her and the child. Oh, not for a moment had she believed he would have allowed her to take Nicky away, but somehow he had figured forcing the choice on her was a good risk.

She could have done one of three things: gone against her feelings for what was right for Nicky and claimed her intention of returning to England with him; insisted on returning alone and hurting Nicky with her apparent rejection of him; or agreed to stay. The first would have put Andros in a bad light with the boy, because he would doubtlessly have blocked it, but he would have lost no credit by the other two choices. She wondered which the influence of those near-black eyes had been willing her to make.

Later, when dinner had been eaten in silence and coffee served in the adjoining lounge, she asked bluntly, 'You were hoping I'd elect to go back to London and refuse to take Nicky, weren't you?'

His eyes flicked up from lighting a cigarette to fix on her and his dark straight brows lifted quizzically.

'What makes you think that?'

'It's obvious,' she snapped at the mild incredulity in his voice, and then, remembering her resolution to avoid unnecessary conflict, she muted her own tone to say, 'I can understand you don't find it easy to share your home with a stranger.'

'Don't I?' Its drawled challenge implied that she was being presumptuous about what he felt. 'Considering the differences in our backgrounds, Alex Saunders, I imagined we were getting along remarkably well ... until yesterday.'

Too well, Alex now saw as she retorted, 'Perhaps you imagined too much, Mr Kontos.'

He laughed shortly at her prim put-down, but he interpreted the concern behind it.

'Do not worry, Alex,' he stressed his use of her first name, making it clear that he wasn't about to revert to addressing her formally, 'I didn't believe you were inviting my ... advances with your occasional smiles. Last night, I did what *I* wanted to do, almost regardless of your wishes.'

She hadn't anticipated his frankness and she dearly hoped the heat she felt fan her cheeks wasn't too obvious a blush. Striving to sound cool, she muttered, 'It was a test, wasn't it?'

'A test?' He seemed genuinely surprised by the idea as he scrutinised her expression through a thin veil of cigarette smoke. 'Is that how you treated it ... at the beginning?'

When she had responded, he meant, and it was Alex's turn to be surprised by the absence of his more usual arrogance. She had thought that through the experience his sensual arousal of her body revealed, he would have known she had been in a state beyond rationality until he had scared her with his own apparent lack of control.

Tempted to give a face-saving 'yes', she felt it safer to reply, 'I'd sooner we forgot all about it, if you don't mind.'

'You brought it up,' he pointed out, 'however obliquely.'

'Well, now I'm dropping it!' Alex bristled with irritation.

'Not yet, I'd prefer to clear it first,' Andros overruled smoothly. 'I don't wish you to be nervous around me.'

'I'm not!' she denied, avoiding his eyes.

'You are wrong in your assumption that I wish you to abandon Nicky while he still needs you. Now you have decided to remain, it is important you realise I shall not take advantage of the fact to force myself on you in any way.'

It sounded so 'terribly honourable', Alex almost laughed aloud, but she stifled the impulse. It was as well, because his taut expression told her he was quite serious.

She answered in the same vein, 'I'm sure you won't.'

'I'm pleased to have your confidence,' he murmured back.

Now that was definitely mocking, Alex discerned, as his mood shifted with an unsettling speed. Had he thought there was a double edge in *her* comment?

Intent on making it clear that she was not issuing any challenges, she enlarged, 'Whatever the reasons for what happened, I'm not so conceited to take it as meaning anything. I *know* you won't try anything like that again.'

'You know, do you?' he repeated her emphatic claim, a thin humourless smile spreading on his mouth. 'You are either incredibly naïve, Alex, or unaware of your power of attraction.'

'I'm not being naïve or modest,' she denied adamantly, 'I'm simply stating that I know you need someone like me in your life about as little as . . .'

'You need me,' he said when she failed to finish it, and there was a hardening in his eyes as well as his voice, before they swept over Alex, perched on the end of his plush velvet sofa, fresh and slim in her blue cotton dungarees and yellow tee-shirt. 'You are right, of

course, you are much too young for my taste, not to
mention your boyish clothing and your stunningly
insolent manners.'

'Thanks,' she muttered acidly.

He shrugged, but there was a hint of a suppressed
smile on his lips when he added, 'I was merely agreeing
with your unsuitability.'

And making her appear a bad-mannered schoolgirl,
in sharp contrast to the way he had made her feel last
night. Her mouth set stubbornly as she veered away
from the memory, but she was brought right back to it
by his next speech.

'That does not say I do not find you sexually
attractive when I forget those factors,' he remarked
urbanely.

If that was consolation he could keep it, Alex fumed
as she reminded him of at least one of those condemning
factors with her impudent response of, 'That's big of you!'

But he seemed oblivious of its rudeness as, head at an
angle, he studied her and came back with, 'I simply
wish to underline that I've promised not to *force* myself
on you, nothing else.'

The banter had disappeared from his voice as his
deep, darkly-fringed eyes caught and held hers, but
Alex refused to take the intention in them seriously. He
was trying to disconcert her, that was all.

And succeeding, she allowed, as again she was the
first to lower her gaze. It alighted on a silver box on the
coffee table and, feeling uncomfortable with the sudden
silence, she asked, 'Can I have one of your cigarettes?'

'You don't have to ask,' he replied a trifle
impatiently, and was awarded another quick resentful
glance for it. When she made no move to take one, he
proffered the open box towards her until she did.
Resuming his seat after lighting her cigarette, he
queried astutely, 'Is that what's bothering you, Alex—
your lack of independence?'

'Partly,' she said, less bitterly than she might have if
he had phrased it as 'your dependence on me', as well

he might. Indeed she went as far as admitting, 'Apart from the few hours I spend with Nicky during the day, I have very little to do besides read and sunbathe.'

'You are bored?' he said as though the notion had never occurred to him.

'Wouldn't you be?' she flipped back, although she doubted he would see it as a fair comparison, and he made no comment on it as he lapsed into thoughtful silence.

Finally he offered, 'It would help, perhaps, if I provided you with some sort of an allowance?'

'No!' Alex was plainly appalled by the idea.

'I can afford it,' he said with a wryness that told her it was a matter of little consequence to him.

It wasn't to Alex. 'That's not the point. I don't want your money—I never did.'

'I realise that now,' he declared, taking Alex completely aback with its quiet certainty, 'although you gave a good pretence of it the first evening we met.'

There was no sting in the comment, but Alex answered defensively all the same, 'I was telling you what you wanted to hear. You weren't giving me much option to do otherwise, if you remember.'

'I remember,' he granted, but qualified it with, 'You were giving quite a performance yourself at the time.'

'What do you mean?' she flashed back.

He stared at her for a long moment, but in the end shrugged, 'Nothing particular.'

But there had been something very pointed in the remark, very penetrating in his look, so much so that Alex blurted out, 'You know, don't you?'

'Know what?' The quick frown etched on his high forehead was just as convincing.

It quelled Alex's sudden shock of suspicion. Her imagination was working overtime. Of course he didn't know. She wouldn't be here now if he knew how much she had deceived him. And when he did?

Strangely Alex was driven on by the pulse of fear that beat hard and strong in her veins as she contemplated

his reaction. Compelled to prove she could overcome
that growing fear of his displeasure, she finally
announced, 'I didn't tell you the whole truth at the
beginning,' and awaited the inevitable cross-examina-
tion.

'Now that does surprise me,' he said eventually on a
dry, sarcastic note as he pushed out of his armchair and
moved towards the door. By the time Alex had broken
free of her frozen incredulity his footsteps were
resounding on the stone tiling in the hall.

She caught up with him as he reached his study off
the corridor that ran through the centre of the large
house. He wheeled round as she stopped him crossing
the threshold. His eyes had never been colder or harder,
and Alex, dropping her hand away from his jacket
sleeve, had to swallow to unblock a dry throat.

'I have to tell you something . . . *now*,' she stressed—
thinking 'now or never'.

He was slow to give an answer, and it was as cold
and disdainful as his gaze. 'It would be a reason for
your leaving Greece, yes?'

'I think so,' she replied, her voice descending to a
shamefully nervous whisper.

'Then you keep your truth, Alex Saunders, I don't
need it,' he dismissed so harshly that she shrank back a
pace. 'You have made a promise to the boy and I'm not
letting you break it. Between us, that is all that matters,
you understand?'

CHAPTER NINE

THE sky was a grey blanket of cloud, the sea flecked white on green. The first dull day in the season, and Alex, slumped on the wicker chair on her balcony, was touched by its gloom. Better than any date on a calendar, it forced her to admit that the prolonged Greek summer was finally ending and to ask the question, why am I still here?—already knowing no answer would satisfy.

She could always use the excuse that *he* had not yet told her to leave, but that would be conceding that he had some right to govern her actions—or worse, that she no longer had the will to defy him.

And yes, the prospect of arriving back in England without a job or place to live was hardly an incentive to leave, but it would have to be faced some time.

Or there was Nicky—but his need for her reassurance grew less frequent as September slipped by and his increasing fluency in Greek helped him overcome initial problems in the mainland school; whispered confidences of how much he dreaded the other boys' teasing giving way to bright chatter about Mino or Ari or one of the other numerous new friends he made.

The confident, sturdy youngster with the dark brown skin was scarcely recognisable as the pale thin boy who had arrived from England with her, and although pleased that he was becoming a robust and lively child, Alex was saddened at the disappearance of even one small trace of her frail, gentle sister in the boy.

She remembered the occasion she had so adamantly claimed Nicky as English to his uncle (such a claim would be laughable now) and wondered if Andros had, from the outset, determined to make it so.

Alex gave a mental shrug that was becoming a habit

over any speculation about his motives. Who knew with any certainty what was really going on behind those dark intelligent eyes? *She* didn't, no matter how long she had spent puzzling over his behaviour since that day of bitter quarrelling over two months ago.

And all that time on, his approach to her had changed so dramatically that she knew she just had to leave before she . . .

Her pride made her skate away from the unfinished thought. Straightening in her chair, she ordered herself to concentrate on the means of her departure rather than reasons. It wasn't difficult—a reservation to make, a suitcase to pack, and a plane to catch—and any day would do.

'So you'll make it soon,' she told herself sternly, and then almost immediately lapsed back into pondering over the recent past.

She wouldn't forget the tension that first week after her attempt to leave—not trusting his cool restrained front; waiting with a restless apprehension for his manner to change once more.

Then one evening when she was preparing herself for another meal in strained silence, he sent a maid to her bedroom to ask if she could join him in the study before dinner. A polite summons, Alex judged, as she dragged her feet downstairs. She had never been inside his private sanctuary before—and it seemed like an ominous first as he called out for her to enter.

She crossed the deep brown carpet to sit on the edge of a straight-backed chair and, avoiding his direct gaze, took in her surroundings. It was a fairly large room with two old-fashioned winged armchairs flanking an unlit fire. His enormous leather-topped desk dominated the far window end.

From experience Alex felt like a schoolgirl in the headmaster's office—an impression which, to her amazement, was almost confirmed when he actually placed a sheet of paper in front of her and asked abruptly, 'Can you translate that?'

Alex quelled any wayward amusement and obediently played out the scene as she ran an eye over the neat typescript.

'Yes, I think so,' she nodded.

'Preferably out loud,' he murmured, a half-smile blunting his sarcastic tone. And when she began to comply, he relaxed to nod and smile fully at her. Despite this close attention, Alex controlled both her nervousness and curiosity to produce a creditable performance.

'That was quite a good first attempt,' he said, after she had finished. 'In fact, almost word-perfect.'

'Almost?' she queried, not understanding how he could judge until he came round to lean on the desk and hand over the paper he himself had been perusing. It was an English translation of the Italian she had just been reading.

She spotted only one mistake—she had read 'cost-efficient' for 'cost-effective'—and then slid him a resentful glance. She'd translated it to be *helpful* to him!

'Shame, I don't get my gold star,' she muttered offhandedly, scorning his silly test.

'I wasn't amusing myself,' he told her, and reached round for a thick wad of typed sheets to fan them for her inspection. 'The rest has not been translated.'

'So?' she prompted when his pause looked as though it was going to develop into a lengthy appraisal.

He looked away. 'So I wondered if you'd be interested in the work—for a fee, of course.'

For a few moments Alex was simply stunned. 'Why?' she asked at last, her sharpness registered by the eyes narrowing back on her face. 'Why do you want *me* to translate it? You must have someone who does this sort of thing for you, and I wouldn't be able to translate it into Greek.'

'Firstly it is for an American, so it must be in English, and secondly, yes, I do employ several translators, but none with English as their native language. As well as accuracy, I require the document to read smoothly.' Placing the folder within her reach, he withdrew to his chair, leaving Alex to breathe easier without him looming over her. More casually he added, 'If you are interested, let's say ... fifteen hundred pounds, and a bonus of five hundred pounds if you finish in six weeks.'

Alex had little idea of her commercial worth as a linguist, and the sum made her gasp. She lifted the document on to her lap and sifted through the pages, most at least three-quarters filled with script. There was definitely a good deal of work in it—but fifteen hundred pounds? She would have done it for a lot less just as a challenge.

She replaced the folder on the desk, saying, 'If it's because I said I was bored then I'd sooner pass—even at that fee.'

It came out more stiff and ungracious than she'd meant, and drew a note of annoyance in his next words of, 'The idea may have been encouraged by your obvious restlessness, but the work is, I assure you, not contrived—nor the sum more than I would have to pay on outside contract.' Her unspoken objections were dealt with in brisk terms. Then he went on to disclose, 'I have a chain of hotels in southern Italy which I am considering selling. This is a report on their operation for a prospective buyer—the American I mentioned. The easier he finds it to assimilate, the more attracted he will be. Apart from that one mistake, your translation had the same sense as the one prepared by one of my employees but sounded more natural to me. So, will you do it?'

'Yes,' Alex grabbed at what was clearly a last chance, but with Andros knowing nothing about her language degree, she couldn't help adding, 'If it's that important, are you sure you want to take a risk on me?'

'What risk?' A shrug dismissed any. 'Lucia tells me your Italian is extremely fluent and I myself know how ... *articulate* your English can be. No, I have total confidence in your ability,' he concluded, a genuine ring to the response that more than compensated for the slight mockery beforehand, and had her flushing with involuntary pleasure. 'I only hope you will find the task absorbing.'

'Oh, I *will*,' she said on an eager note, and took no exception to his quick smile at her enthusiasm. It was more indulgent than condescending, and now she was no longer looking for any devious motives behind his offer, she recalled how ungrateful she must have appeared in the beginning. She tried to make up for it with, 'And thank you for considering me. It was very . . . kind of you.'

There was no doubting the wry twist on his lips for her hesitancy, but when she tried a conciliatory smile on him, it was answered with a full dazzling charm that made her catch her breath with its suddenness. And before she could recover, he was guiding her through to dinner and making it clear their period of silence was over.

The strange unexpected interview had been a turning point. For, from it, Andros became less critical of her casual ways—more tolerant of her unsophisticated manner. And Alex responded by keeping her tongue under control and tacitly avoiding taboo subjects.

There appeared to be three main ones. She was not to refer to her eventual departure—he clearly viewed this as his decision. She mustn't broach the subject of her life in England (he was still as angrily stubborn about not wanting to know details). And the third . . . well, that one seemed the most unreasonable.

It concerned Mario. It transpired that the Italian boy was not so much a chauffeur as a general assistant. While Andros had lived on the mainland, Mario had a couple of rooms in the village, and a staff room available to him in the Athens hotel. Mainly he kept the villa on the hillside stocked with fresh food, maintained its swimming pool and exterior ground, and fetched a woman from the village twice a week to clean the inside. When the villa had been closed up his duties were reduced so most days he now reported to the island in his own small boat.

A hard worker herself, Lucia his mother, hated to see her lanky, ever-grinning son idle. One afternoon, unable to find anything at all to keep him occupied, she had the inspiration that the young English girl might appreciate a visit to the village to do some shopping.

At first Alex had demurred. Apart from the fact she was heavily engrossed in the translation, instinct told her Andros would not approve. Recently he had been taking Nicky and herself out in the speeedboat in the evenings. Skirting the mainland coastline, he was a fast but skilful driver, and he caused Alex to thrill at the feel of wind and speed as much as the dramatic hill scenery rising from the shore. Although they never landed and Alex had not, in fact, been on any other soil than the four square miles of Armina since arriving, she was strangely reluctant to jeopardise these sorties just for a trip to the village.

So it was against her better judgment she allowed herself to be persuaded to go—less by Lucia's motherly concern over the time she spent scribbling on paper and hammering away at a typewriter in the library than Nicky's determined badgering for Dimitri, Lucia's younger son, and himself to be included in any expedition. But at her request Mario took them east to the town of Sariso on one of the larger islands nearby.

The weather was glorious and the town was teeming with tourists off the ferryboats. It was noisy and boisterous after the peace in Armina. The boys spent some time admiring the boats in the larger harbour, then wandering through the open street markets.

Alex was content to browse, careful not to show too much interest in the local pottery and jewellery she could not afford. She had a little Greek money Andros had not confiscated; a few pounds' worth she had found in the jacket she had worn to travel from London, and Mario obviously expected her to buy something, so she chose a blue polka-dot headscarf to prevent her hair getting into such a tangle on the speedboat journey. The rest she blew on some enormous ice cream sundaes and, watching Mario dispose of his, she decided she really had three boys in her charge.

Afterwards they followed some music to the town square where a band was playing. Dressed in traditional embroidered tunics and billowing white trousers, they provided a fast tempo for the dancers who threaded skilfully through the famous 'Zorba' dance. The males in the crowd were encouraged to join in, and soon Mario and Dimitri were absorbed in the morass of gesticulating people. Nicky stood hesitatingly at her side, looking enviously on but so plainly feeling he should stay with her.

Sensing his dilemma and perhaps the right time for another talk, Alex took his hand and led him away from the crowd. They couldn't go far because of the others, but she sat him down on a low wall of the church they had passed at the far corner of the square.

'Listen, Nicky, you won't be asked to make that choice again—between the island and ...' she paused and changed from saying 'and me' to '... and London. You can't go back there, love, because it just isn't right for you—all that moving around from flat to flat, and the damp weather, and never having a garden to play in. That's why Mummy told you about the island, remember? She knew you'd be better here. She knew you'd be coming home as Daddy always wanted you to do. And *I* know you wouldn't be happy anywhere else now, Nick. So be happy for me, and stay?'

He nodded solemnly but returned, not surprisingly, 'Will you, Lex?'

His eyes were bright with appeal and Alex wished she could have answered with the desired promise, could have disregarded its impossibility. Her silence was telling and so was Nicky's changing expression, as he resigned himself to disappointment. This time Nicky would accept what she had to say more broodingly than dramatically. She put her arm round his shoulder and pulled him closer.

'I'll always love you, Nicky, you must believe that,' she spoke quietly, but there was a wealth of love and affection in her voice, 'and if I could, I'd like to be with you but, try and see, this life isn't right for me. I don't feel Greek like you do, and I'm too old to change. It's just not . . . not home to me, Nick.'

He took it with a long silence and then said with an anxiety that was so unselfish she was almost crushed by it, 'But without me, you'll be on your own, Lex.'

'Oh, Nick boy, don't worry about me,' she chided, but cancelling any reprimand with a rough hug.

'You'll come back and see me?' He was crying a little now, but he seemed to be squaring up to the inevitable.

'Or you'll come and see me,' she affirmed with the confidence of knowing that if Nicky wanted to enough, Andros would agree. 'It's going to be all right, Nicky, you'll see,' she added, squeezing his shoulders.

He began to scrub his tears away when Mario and Dimitri appeared in view. 'But you'll stay a bit longer, Lex?' he urged quickly before the other two could arrive.

'A little while,' she agreed but then thought it too vague. Based on the work she had yet to do for Andros, she specified, 'About a month more, right?'

He was going to cope, Alex determined as she watched him, one minute gravely nodding back at her, and the next, racing around the edge of the crowd after Dimitri. She was glad of it, but it hurt all the same.

Hiding her emotions behind the bright smile she gave Mario, she returned to the harbour.

If she could have foreseen their reception back on the island some hours on, Alex might have vastly reduced her one month estimate.

True, it was very late in the afternoon when they returned and the boys did look less than immaculate—

but it was hardly *her* fault that the boat's engine wouldn't start or that the boys had made messy assistants to Mario's rather inept mechanic before they had been given a hand by another boat-owner.

No, but Alex saw she was going to get the blame no matter what she said, as she climbed out of the boat last and joined the rest of the group already undergoing Andros's furious inspection. And from his attitude, it didn't look like she was going to get much chance to say anything.

Her nervousness turned abruptly to indignation when he shouted Nicky down before the boy got out more than a tentative, 'Hello, Uncle Ros,' and ordered him to bath and then bed. It spoke a lot for Nicky's spirit that he dared to consult Alex with a 'what have I done?' look, but he didn't need another telling after Andros roared, 'Now, boy!'

Dimitri was smart enough to include himself in the dictate and took to his heels as well, which left Mario, shocked and scared by his first experience of any unreasonable temper from his idol, and Alex, defiant and plainly fuming at the bullying way he had just treated Nicky.

'You shouldn't have . . .'

'Shut up!' she was told with biting arrogance and momentarily ignored while he turned on Mario.

After weeks in the mainly Greek household, she could understand most of Andros's harsh speech, and guess the less familiar words by their inflection. Mario was getting his wrists slapped, or more aptly, his hands sliced off, for daring to take her anywhere off the island without his permission.

Alex wouldn't have thought any less of Mario if he had disappeared in his own boat the moment Andros's tirade was over, but she thought a lot more of him as, clearly afraid of the older man's anger, he didn't desert her without a qualm. When Andros repeated his dismissal and shot him a dark warning look from beneath thunderous brows, he stood his ground first having shifted slightly so that he was between Andros and herself.

Alex would have liked to applaud the gesture but had an awful vision of what might result. She interceded quickly, some rapid Italian and a careless glance in Andros's direction convincing Mario she could handle the situation.

She did not fool herself. Mario had barely turned over his outboard and swung the tiller to make a wide sweep of the bay when Andros attacked.

'What did you say to him?' he rapped out.

Alex didn't see that it mattered, but she relayed faithfully, 'I told him you were miffed because you wanted to take Nicky out somewhere and that you'd calm down when you saw you were making a fuss over nothing.'

It was debatable whether he knew the exact nuance of 'miffed', but he must have certainly understood that she was telling him he had overreacted. Her offhand tone, however, was no appeal to reason.

'Where were you?' he barked back, blocking her path almost before she moved. 'And don't lie. You weren't at the village as Lucia thinks, because I was there earlier.'

'So I wasn't at the village,' Alex shrugged. 'I didn't realise I was living on Alcatraz, otherwise I might have made good my escape,' she quipped, provoked by his assumption that she would lie.

He was not amused, but the anger blazing in his eyes cooled to icy control as he admitted, 'I thought you had.'

'Oh!' She saw the light. It wasn't very pleasant. 'You're mad because I came back?' she enquired, purely sarcastic.

He didn't need to supply the harsh rider of, 'And taken the boy.'

But Alex didn't consider it as justification for his temper now. Her laugh was short and derisive. 'For future reference, how was I going to manage that without any money and with Mario in tow?'

'You're resourceful,' he muttered, making it sound less than a compliment. 'With your talents, Miss Saunders, I'm sure you could have persuaded Mario to help you.'

Here we go again, Alex thought, registering the use of her surname and the slur in his tone. For a second she was tempted to play up by agreeing that she found Mario a very eager and willing young man—but she hesitated about involving him.

In the end she declared with exaggerated patience, 'Look, let's leave Mario out of this. Yes, perhaps by some means I could have managed it, but I didn't even consider it. Why can't you accept that I'll be leaving Nicky with you and be a good winner about it?'

His eyes narrowed on her face. 'Perhaps because you don't make me feel I'm winning,' he replied, more enigmatic than angry, and Alex could only assume he meant her attitude didn't inspire trust.

'I can't help that.' She wasn't going out of her way to convince him and hoped it would conclude the argument. It didn't.

'Where were you?' he repeated his original question in a slightly more civilised tone and noting her stubborn expression, added, 'I can always ask Nicky.'

'I think you've terrified him enough for one day, don't you?' She couldn't resist the dig and knew she'd scored a point by the tightening of his lips. Feeling generous on it, she admitted almost appeasingly, 'Nowhere special. Just to Sariso.'

'Why?' he demanded with an immediate suspicion.

'Why?—I don't believe this!' she exclaimed shooting him an exasperated glance for what she thought was a silly, unnecessary question. 'You'd have been a great asset to the Spanish Inquisition!'

'Alex!' He might have reverted to using her first name, but there was a threatening ring to it, as he gritted his teeth.

'All right, we went to visit the town there. The boys had a look at the ferryboats in the harbour. I had a few drachma you missed on the first day and I bought this scarf from a market stall.' She pulled the polka-dot square off and tossed her hair back with a dramatic defiant flourish. 'We had some ice cream in a café. Afterwards Mario and Dimitri joined in some dancing in the town square. When we decided to come home, the boat wouldn't start at first, so we're late,' she exhausted the day's events on a studiously bored rather than apologetic note, and compounded it with, 'In case you don't realise, it's what ordinary people call enjoying themselves.'

'Don't be insolent!' he instructed with a deep scowl, every bit the grim autocrat Alex had intended to imply.

She restrained an impulse to snap to attention and waited in sullen silence for the next question to be fired at her. Instead she had to suffer his steady brooding stare.

'Can I go?' she muttered, taking his reply as read.

'Not yet.' A hand shot out as she made to pass him and held her fast at his side, his fingers biting into her arm.

'I suppose you know you're hurting me,' she protested, clenching her teeth—it was the nearest she was going to come to asking for mercy, and she herself was surprised when he yielded, slackening his grip almost instantly.

But she was left gasping at his reply of, 'I suppose you never hurt me, English girl.'

'*Me?* ... Hurt *you?*' she scorned, the nerve of him suggesting she deserved his brutality. 'You're head of the Kontos empire, remember? Lord of all we survey. Absolute ruler in your own little island kingdom. How could I possibly hurt you?'

'You really don't know?' His sharp laugh of disbelief said she did, and Alex wondered for a few seconds if she had missed something.

'I *really don't know*,' she laboured each word, having decided he was just trying to put her on the defensive. 'Do enlighten me. I'd love to know where your Achilles' heel is.' Alex half expected retribution for the flippancy, certainly not the sudden wry smile with which he greeted the remark. Somehow she had pleased him without intending to.

'No, I don't think that would be a good idea,' he murmured, shaking his head at her. 'Clever little Alex, on instinct alone, your aim is viciously accurate.'

'Thanks,' she muttered at what was scarcely a flattering comment despite the admiring way it had been delivered. 'You're too kind.'

'Not at all,' he mocked her very English dryness. 'You deserve every word.'

'I wish I could believe that,' she drawled back, and meant it too. Why should the power to hurt be all his? But wishing it different didn't shake her conviction of his invulnerability. Cynically she added, 'Next time I draw blood, you'll have to show me. I'd be fascinated.'

'Blood from a rock, no?' He smiled while Alex visibly recovered from the surprise of him both knowing the expression and being able to read it from her mind.

'From a stone, actually,' she corrected, lips tightening. 'And you said it, not me.'

He slanted her an appraising look. 'But you don't regard me as very human, do you?'

'I don't think I'll risk answering that,' she returned cagily, not sure where she was being led.

'I'll keep my temper.' He offered her a smile that made him look like a man who never lost it, but Alex's memory wasn't that short.

'Is that a promise?' Her tone suggested that even if it were, she wouldn't trust it.

'I'd write it in blood, but . . .' His mouth curved with humour, and when Alex's own features relaxed slightly he asked, 'How *do* you see me, Alex?'

It was possible he was seeking a straight answer despite the banter beforehand, but Alex didn't want to give one. After consideration she offered, 'Oh, like one of your ancient gods from mythology, I think.'

He gave her a wry glance, having picked up the heavy

irony in her voice, and commented, 'I don't feel I'm about to be flattered. Dare I ask which one?'

'I haven't decided yet,' she murmured back, making a pretence of studying his overly handsome face before proving how cutting she could be. 'It's so difficult to choose—they were all a pretty cruel and vengeful bunch to us lesser mortals.'

Her smile of satisfaction froze on her lips as she watched the fine dark head thrown back with the force of his laughter. She had just insulted him. *She* knew she had. She began to wonder if *he* did.

'What's so funny?' she demanded crossly when he faced her again, his lips still twitching with amusement.

'You!' he admitted succinctly, and Alex who had already suspected that, positively glared at him. He raised his hands in a pacifying attitude before he went on, 'I'm sorry, but if I find my deification under your terms as offensive as it was undoubtedly intended to be, your identifying yourself with the "lesser mortals" has to be the absurdest thing I've ever heard.'

'I don't see why,' Alex objected sulkily, feeling very much the disadvantaged underdog.

'In all the mythology I've ever read, most of the lesser mortals had a healthy respect for their gods. They recognised their power and they knew when to heed their wrath,' he pointed out dryly. 'Whereas you, my stubborn proud Alex, would be still arguing back *after* the thunderbolt struck,' he finished on a highly amused note.

'And that bothers you, doesn't it? That I won't take your bullying lying down?' she challenged, tilting her head with spirit and making an unconsciously lovely picture for the man gazing down at her.

'I must admit,' he returned in a quiet, musing tone, 'that your taking . . . something from me lying down has some appeal.'

His meaning sank in as he smiled at her with a lazy satisfaction, and at last Alex was rendered speechless, for the innuendo stirred a too clear memory of that night on the beach. Worse, she was convinced they shared the same thoughts for his expression was very knowing. Contemptuous as she was of his words she didn't seem able to drag her eyes away from his—say any of the indignant things she felt she should be saying.

'There was, of course, another kind of relationship a god might have with a mortal if she were beautiful,' he continued in the same tone, but his words were soft and seductive now, 'And then the cruellest, most vengeful of gods would turn into the gentlest, most loving of worshippers. We could try it that way, beautiful Alex.'

'No, don't ...' It was a shamefully weak protest against the hand trailing down her heated cheek to curve on the soft skin of her neck.

'Why not?' He traced the pulse at the base of her neck beating so strongly at his light destructive touch. 'It's the way it should be between us, Alex.'

'I ... I don't see that,' she denied with a slow helpless shake of her head—then went rigid with shock as he slipped his hand between her blouse and skin.

He removed it almost immediately, perhaps conscious of being overlooked by the house, but only after he had spread his hard palm against her breast and drawn an involuntary gasp of pleasure as one finger fleetingly touched its sensitive peak.

'Your body seems to know it,' he murmured, as his hand returned to circle her upper arm.

Even Alex felt it a little late for verbal reproaches, too late to make any violent moves. Her body, trembling like a leaf in the gentlest of winds, seemed to support his quiet claim.

It took an effort to articulate, 'No, *you* know it—how to make my body respond like that, I mean,' and sounded so unlike herself, so nervous and uncertain, that his next comment was understandable.

'Come, Alex, you're not a shy virgin I am trying to take advantage of,' he said, his wryness suggesting he wouldn't be interested in her if she were. 'Or are you telling me you would respond like that for any man who knew the right moves?'

'No, I wouldn't!' Alex found herself exclaiming with some of her usual spirit and then shut her eyes in self-despair at his soft laugh.

She only heard the sweet savage note in his, 'Good, I might have strangled you if the answer had been yes,' but her eyes were startled open by the light kiss brushed on her brow and held by his tender gaze as his voice became even more pervasive, 'And it would be beautiful between us, Alex, I promise. The differences you feel just wouldn't matter if we were lovers.'

At first Alex simply stared at him in fascination. He means it, she thought, he really means it.

But it just didn't seem real. In all seriouness was he suggesting they become lovers? With rapt attention was she actually listening to him? They both had to be crazy. She said so, but not in anger against him.

'Andros, you can't believe that really,' she started, unsure if she was asking him or telling him. 'Not fifteen minutes ago you were yelling at me and I was being insolent right back. And now you say we could be ... well, it makes no sense. It wouldn't work ...'

And why in God's name am I justifying turning down his proposition as if it was a marriage proposal? Alex asked herself as she faltered to a grinding halt.

'It is not unusual for a man and woman to argue a little at the beginning of a relationship,' he said with a slight smile, and Alex gaped at him for a couple of seconds.

'We don't *argue*, Andros, we *fight*,' she stated emphatically, but he ignored the comment as though he hadn't heard it.

'It can normally be put down to strong attraction coupled with physical frustration,' he smoothly finished his explanation.

'*I'm* not frustrated!'

'Then *you* are lucky.' His smile was sardonic. 'But you *are* attracted,' he added as she quivered at his running a hand down her arm in a featherlight stroke.

They seemed to have come full circle, and this time Alex thought better of denying it.

'That's not enough,' she rejected impulsively. 'I wouldn't get involved with someone just because of a purely physical response. On both sides there'd have to be ...'

'Love?' Andros supplied with a mocking twist.

She supposed that was what she had been hesitating to say—and small wonder, for she could have predicted his cynicism especially in view of the wild impressions she had earlier fostered about her sex life—in reality confined to fending off a few clumsy passes at the occasional student party.

'You need to be *told* you are loved, is that it?' he made it sound like a typically female weakness, 'Because, Alex, if it's important to you, then I ...'

'Don't waste your breath!' Alex cried out before he could say more. 'For your information, Andros Kontos, it's how *I* feel that's important to me. I wouldn't need a lie to sway me into doing what *I* wanted. But *you* could tell me you loved me till I grew old hearing it, and I'd never even *want* to believe it, far less let myself be seduced by it like the obviously stupid women you're used to talking into your bed,' she ended the angry speech on a high note of defiance.

'Are you quite finished?' he asked coldly while she remained sullen and silent. 'Good, because for *your information*, Alex Saunders, I was about to say that I couldn't, in all honesty, tell you what I feel for you is love, and it isn't my style to pretend otherwise,' he relayed in a very convincing tone. 'And if *stupid* women are my style,' he slanted her a considering look that warned her what was coming, 'I wouldn't be too sure I won't talk *you* into my bed one day.'

'I ...' Alex began a stammering response, but Andros had decided his was to be the last word.

'For now, I'll be patient,' he continued smoothly, as though he were giving her a concession, and then made clear what he expected in return, 'But, Alex, stay away from Mario. Your spirit of rebellion seems to be spreading, and while I might look forward to taming it in you, I don't like it in the boy. And if you're a good girl,' he patted her cheek, 'I'll take you places myself.'

Then having made her appear about five years old and a half-wit into the bargain, he wandered off along the jetty, leaving Alex wanting to scream with frustration and knowing too well he would just love to hear it.

CHAPTER TEN

'Not one of my more glorious moments,' Alex reflected as her thoughts returned from the events which had prompted that third taboo.

'Thou shalt not corrupt Mario,' she murmured aloud, and despite the inherent insult, she had to give a wry smile when she considered who had issued the commandment. For if Andros Kontos resembled any god—and how she wished that analogy had never occurred to her—it was definitely the pagan variety.

Oh, he'd kept his promise and taken her places—whether she liked it or not. Within a week he had procured a power launch more suitable for longer journeys than a speedboat. Naturally Nicky had been captivated by the boat, and she had had to hide her own admiration on the tour of inspection Andros insisted she have. It was all polished walnut and gleaming brass on the upper deck, compact and functional fittings below, but with touches of luxury that would have made it no hardship to live on it permanently. When Andros had explained that he had borrowed the sleek expensive boat for a few weeks from a friend, Alex had smiled at the thought—'well, what are friends for, after all?'

But the next day she had refused to take part in its trial run to nearby Kea. For some things she had a long memory, and his 'if you're a good girl' had still been ringing in her ears, despite his deceptively pleasant attitude since that had made all her attempts at aloofness seem like childish sulking.

She had ended up going, of course, but only after he had blackmailed her by telling Nicky with a disgusting semblance of sincerity that he himself didn't feel like making the trip either without her company.

But if she had given in to the little boy's wheedling, she had given little of her *precious* company to Andros that time.

On longer trips to the Cyclades Islands in the south, however, with Lucia's husband, Spiro, along to share the steering, it was impossible to avoid Andros; and sometimes just as difficult to remember reasons why she should.

For yes, he had been patient—as patient as any hunter stalking a prey with the sense not to stand still too long for him. His touches were the most casual—an arm resting briefly on her shoulder as they stood at the boat's railing to greet the shore coming into view; his hand guiding her while the boys scrambled ahead among the ancient ruins on Naxos and Tinos; his body briefly close to hers when she had failed to get the hang of windsurfing, and like a conscientious teacher he had helped her to the surface. And with them, soft words and looks that told her what he wanted from her.

At first it had been all right. She had thought it a game the way he had played it and felt herself safe in knowing it was one. When he had sought to charm, she would give him baleful glances that told him he wasn't succeeding, and he would laugh as if to say he was at least enjoying the trying. She supposed it had amused her too—it had almost seemed, at times, to be a shared joke between them. Perhaps she had been a little flattered—even if his intentions were strictly dishonourable. And sometimes when they would share a day of easy laughing companionship, she would catch herself remembering that strange promise of how it would be if they were lovers, and not think it so strange any more.

But if she had indulged in the occasional daydream about Andros and known she grew more rather than less attracted as time went by, she had still seen herself as firmly in control of the situation. After all, only a fool would have taken such a game seriously.

'And you were so sure you weren't that,' Alex murmured to herself, and raised a hand to brush away some tears.

It was a cross gesture. She didn't know why she had to keep crying about it. Nothing had happened, not really. She'd made a little fool of herself. That didn't mean to say she was going to make a big fool of herself. She had to get it into perspective. A small incident where her control had slipped, that was all . . .

She had been at a loose end with Nicky in school and the translation finished the previous week when Andros arrived home unexpectedly early one afternoon. He found her in the library, sitting curled up in the window seat and making heavy weather of a Greek translation of *David Copperfield*, and suggested a visit to an ancient temple along the coast from Lavrian. He made it a very casual-sounding invitation. She thought, why not, and didn't wait around for an answer to occur to her. And that was the first rule of the game disregarded, for Nicky had always been the ostensible reason for their spending any time together.

With just the two of them in the speedboat—the launch had been returned to its owner—Andros allowed her to take the wheel for a while and only took it back at her panicked request. His indulgence for her shortcomings, highlighed by the competence with which he did most things, had grown over the weeks. Some days she resented it. That day she was too pleased with the sudden treat to mind his lazy smile at her meandering course.

They didn't say much on the way towards the ruins, saving their breath for the warm climb up the twisting hill path cut through a tangle of wild vines. The temple was disappointing, little more than a few pillars still standing among the rubble, but Andros invested it with interest, relaying its background, the cycle of construction to various Greek gods and destruction by the Romans, with the footnote that it had been used as a landmark for the landing of British troops in the second world war. With genuine admiration she remarked on his thorough knowledge of its history, only to have him admit he had looked it up beforehand to impress her. There was something very ambiguous in his laughter that gave her the choice whether to be flattered or not, and she shot him a look that called him a shameful liar before she sauntered back towards the beach.

She was going too fast on the twisting dirt path for her open-toed sandals when she stumbled.

He was close behind her when he saved her from falling, and his steadying of her was quite instinctive.

But the rest that followed was very deliberate as together they broke too many rules of the game ever to go back to playing it the same way again.

At the point where Alex had previously pulled herself free of his lingering hold and he would give a soft laugh to mock her haste, some perverse devil made Alex turn slowly at arms' length and stay just where she was. A teasing provocative move, he realised it as such and smiled down into the wide blue eyes challenging him to make *his* move before she inevitably slipped away. That moment it *was* all game for both of them.

Then suddenly the laughter faded—blown away on the breeze that lifted Alex's hair and flicked silky strands out to whip lightly against the face bent towards her. She made to trap her hair, but he told her not to and there was something low and gruff in his tone that both warned her to shy away on the instant and excited her to stay until that last second.

She heeded neither urge when Andros's head began to lower slowly to cut out the sun. Instead she let herself obey an instinct to shut her eyes in silent invitation, and moaned softly as he took her lips on his. At first he was content with that small submission to him and his mouth was warm and playful on hers. Perhaps it would have been enough for him if Alex hadn't had to raise her hands to his shoulders to hold her balance as she grew slightly dizzy. But he took the movement as her willingness to be drawn closer so that she was braced against him and could feel his stirring desire for her as he deepened the kiss.

Then it wasn't enough for either of them as they lost consciousness of both time and place.

At best they must have looked highly incongruous to the two young men appearing round the bend in the path, to find their way blocked by a girl in tee-shirt and denim shorts being almost lifted off the ground by a man obviously much older—so much smarter in suit trousers and slackened tie, with his hands on the curve of her slim back as she strained towards him. Or that was how Alex judged the situation afterwards. They had broken apart and, deprived of the heady excitement of his endless kiss, she came crashing back to earth to register the two grinning young men.

They were both of her generation and, as it turned out, American. For having been awarded one of Andros's dark threatening stares while Alex looked at the ground, one mumbled a hasty, 'Excuse me,' but their voices carried in loud transatlantic drawls as they went on up the path.

'Lucky we weren't five minutes later,' one boy remarked with irony, but his friend was more explicit.

'Pity, you mean. By then the old guy would have been so turned on he wouldn't have noticed if the Boston Philharmonic had walked by!'

The words drifted back to them, and Alex had to hold on to the 'old guy's' arm with a frantic strength. She had little doubt that a tall, muscular Andros could make the skinny teenagers eat their words, but she pleaded with her eyes not to make things worse as the laughing boy continued, 'With a beautiful chick like that hot for you, would you?'

'Uh-huh, not even if they were playing Beethoven's Fifth at the time,' the other chuckled back. 'Did you see the way she was clinging to him—wowee!'

They appeared to have made the young tourists' day and probably were the subject of discussion all the way up the hill. Fortunately any more was lost to them.

Alex dropped her eyes away. She knew her face was aflame with colour. She could have happily died right then—or maybe earlier, when she had been oblivious of everything but Andros's loving and before the boys' comments made her aware of how hungrily she had been responding to it.

She felt sick and cheap, but when she forced her eyes back to his, she prayed he had recovered his laughter. He hadn't. His face was still rigid with anger, and she imagined it must now be with her for instigating the whole scene by not withdrawing when she should have. With his arrogance, he would hate being the butt of the young men's jokes—wouldn't he?

'I'm sorry. It ... it was my fault,' she confessed falteringly, not realising the dark eyes now holding hers weren't accusing.

'Silly girl—you were beautiful.' His hand tilted her chin up, touched one blushing cheek. 'Don't feel shamed. They made it dirty because they were excited—just envying me your young loveliness. You are beautiful, Alex,' he sighed with a look of such tenderness that her heart missed a beat and then several as it acknowledged that nothing could ever be the same between them again.

And nothing was.

Not from that moment when she found herself fighting the crazy impulse to return to his arms but overcame it and turned wordlessly from him. It was obvious she wanted to be alone, and he let her go. Later, at the boat, he said they should talk, but Alex shook her head, knowing herself incapable then of making sense—to Andros least of all. The trip back to the island was conducted in silence.

It set the pattern for the next few days, but it was no longer the oppressive silence between master and chastened servant. Idiotic as it seemed, Alex had just become too conscious of him to say anything natural at all. Mostly she would avoid his eyes, and when she caught them by accident, it was a close-run thing which of them was more anxious to look away.

But she knew he wasn't angry with her, for

occasionally he would break the silence with a curiously mundane question that would require some reply— almost as though he was trying to keep a bare contact going. It was a strange time, and she breathed a heavy sigh of relief when he went away to Italy on business for a week.

There was one small strained conversation the morning he left. She asked if she could have her payment for the translation, and was awarded a long measuring look before he promised it on his return. His perception was fair but not faultless. Rather wearily she repeated that if she was planning on leaving it would be without Nicky.

And he said the strangest thing back—that he would almost prefer it if she took the child with her—and at her shocked expression, stranger still he muttered, 'Because if you did, Alex Saunders, you'd give me reason to track you down and take my revenge any way I could!'

And you'd spin dreams out of that? Alex derided herself, as her mind drifted back from those last words of his.

Only a fool would read any tender feeling into such a threat ... would waste whole days thinking about a man who, if he wanted anything of her, it was to end their battle of wills with her final submission in his bed.

And she wasn't a fool, was she? Not a hundred per cent committed one, at least. She remembered a girl in her French class who had fallen for a medical student and been reduced from a witty intelligent girl to a credulous ninny. Anyone with half an ounce of sense would have seen that the aspiring doctor didn't give a damn, but poor infatuated Marcia had spent whole months wildly interpreting his vagaries as undeclared love and had learned the hard way after he had moved on to sleep with another girl.

No, she was definitely not a Marcia. She knew that if Andros said nasty offensive things to her, it was because he meant them, not due to some secret insecurity complex (Andros Kontos with an insecurity complex was about as convincing as Adolf Hitler with a heart of gold). And if, in between times, he made a few pretty speeches and gave her soft lingering looks, they were undoubtedly intended to be taken seriously—long enough, at any rate, for him to talk her in and out of his bed. As for the pregnant silences—well, they were as likely to signify boredom as anything deep and meaningful. So no, she wasn't in Marcia's league at all.

But was she so much better?—having the wisdom to understand the way it was, yet the foolishness to be still fascinated by Andros. Certainly no more virtuous—realising that any relationship between them would be a mockery of love, corrupt and damned from the very start, but returning over and over to feed on each memory of his touch—until she saw him again.

And then? If she were sane, she'd take her money and run. And if not?

She gave a crooked smile as she wondered how Andros would reconcile her being at least in part a shy virgin, with her being the mother of a six-year-old. Well, he had always wanted to treat Nicky as a divine conception—but she doubted she would convince him of it!

No! There was no point in speculating on maybes, she impatiently dismissed her thoughts, and scooped herself out of the balcony chair to look out the clothes that might require a wash before packing.

She needed to get off his island before she . . . Alex halted almost in shock as she caught some of the madness of what she had been contemplating in the wide-eyed expression she saw in the wardrobe mirror.

And what if he didn't spot her lack of experience?—he would allow her to stick around just long enough for him to make up for it and possibly give her one of his fat pay-off cheques as if she was a whore, and by then she might even take it, because she'd probably be feeling like one. She'd have to be crazy or in love to let herself in for that.

'And you're not in love—so don't forget it,' she told the girl staring doubtfully back at her, anguish in her eyes. Then, recognising it as a near quote, she finished it silently—it's just a silly phase you're going through.

Very silly . . . the girl in the mirror was crying again. Well, she'd be stronger, Alex swore, as she snatched open the door and grabbed a handful of jeans and shirts off their hangers. She'd be ready to leave as dry-eyed and hard-headed as ever.

Late afternoon. And she wasn't ready at all. She should have had another two clear days to sort the clothes cried on and left crumpled on her bed, to arrange her thoughts into a farewell speech of cut and style which might even convince herself.

Instead she was standing on the jetty, her smile for Nicky frozen, her mind screaming 'unfair'. How dare *he* be there next to Spiro—three days early and totally unexpected!

He was drawing closer, catching her eyes, a half-smile forming on his lips, and Alex knew if they talked at all, she wouldn't manage more than a whisper as her feelings rose up to choke her. Her charm phrase diminished to just two words, the only meaningful ones in that first moment when they exchanged looks and she realised herself 'in love' with Andros Kontos.

And crazy with it, for she imagined the same emotion reflected in his eyes, and if they had been alone she would have been in danger of confessing her madness right then and there in that first instant of contact. Fortunately they weren't.

Spiro smiled at her as he passed with Andros's case. Dimitri muttered a cheery hello. Nicky offered his cheek for a kiss and was duly given one. And Alex desperately gathered up her defences.

Then Nicky came out with, 'Aren't you going to kiss Uncle Ros?—he's been away ages!' and her face flamed with colour as she made a poor show of ignoring the comment and Andros's teasing smile. In fact she returned it because she couldn't do anything else. Later she was to think it very fickle of her to turn her back on her sensible half so damned easily.

'For that you deserve a reward, Nicky,' Andros murmured, switching his smile to the little boy for a second, and Nicky grinned back, although he obviously hadn't been cued. 'Why don't you run after Spiro and get him to open up my suitcase and see what's in it?' he added, turning the child and laughingly pushing him in the right direction to chase after the other two.

'Just a little present. There's one for Dimitri as well,' was directed at Alex with a shade of justification.

'That's fine—really,' she mumbled hastily. He had reminded her of their past argument over the toy yacht, and she didn't want reminding. Now she wanted to believe the way he was looking at her, as if he didn't ever want to take his eyes off her face. She knew she was looking back at him in the very same way.

'You missed me,' he said next, and Alex wasn't sure if he was asking or telling her.

But she was proud of herself for even being able to make a joke of it, saying, 'Do *I* get a present if I say yes?'—uncertain if she was flirting or merely trying to appear halfway normal.

'Well, I *have* something for you,' his smile was as secret as a small boy's, 'and that's the answer I want, but the question's slightly different.'

'Oh,' Alex said warily, as her imagination worked on the possible question.

'Come on, let's go for a walk.' He reached for her hand as though it was the most natural thing in the world, and added, like an afterthought she should have taken for granted, 'I missed you, Alex.'

The wind was brisk, flapping at his suit jacket and whipping her hair round her head. Alex felt cold and nervous, even if the hand tightly gripping hers offered warmth and confidence. They didn't walk far, just round to the next cove out of sight of the house, before he turned to face her.

He stretched out a hand to catch her wayward hair so

he could hold it back from her face. Her eyes were wide, and the bluest he had ever seen.

'Do you need to hear the words, Alex?' he asked almost gruffly. 'You must know how I feel.'

Alex continued to stare up at him, reading a confusion of emotions chasing across his fine, saturnine features, unable to tell what was real, and what she had wished there. She shook her head in slow bewilderment. She needed the words—but when she heard them, they confirmed her fears and shattered any small dream scarcely born that first moment they had seen each other again.

'Oh God, how I want you, Alex,' he murmured thickly as his mouth came down on hers.

It wasn't an expert kiss. There was too much feeling in it, too much hunger. In fact it was almost brutal in its lack of control, and if his words hadn't already frightened and hurt Alex with their intense, purely physical demand, his kiss would surely have. It sought to force her to respond, yet gave her little chance to, and perhaps Andros knew it, because when she started to panic and struggle in earnest, he released her with a muffled curse and a groaned apology as she twisted away from him.

Alex might have forgiven him it, and any roughness, if the words had been 'how I love you' or even 'how I need you'. But how I *want* you—it was too near her own judgment of the way it had to be, only he wasn't waiting for the end to give her rewards for being a 'good' girl. And if she had any pride she wouldn't wait till he asked that obvious question.

She knew her own words—she just had to find the strength to articulate them. Strangely he gave it, placing his hands on her shoulders and nuzzling her neck in the gentlest of manners as though it would erase his momentarily unsubtle approach. He was so sure he could manipulate her to his will, and was so close to doing so she felt angry with herself. How could she possibly be in love with such a man?

'At any rate, Andros, I'm glad you're back,' she paused, and her forced laugh was more brittle than even she'd intended, 'I want to go home, and as usual, I need to ask you for some money.'

A second's stillness then she was spun round like a rag doll. 'What are you saying?' It was hoarse with disbelief, and if she had ever managed to hurt him, it was then.

But she dragged her eyes away from sharing that surprising pain in his. He didn't need her sympathy. He didn't need her. *Want*, remember, she drummed into her wavering mind.

'I'm going back to London as soon as possible. You *owe* me some money for that work I did,' she specified more clearly, but he was still shaking his head in denial of anything she might say. She jerked back out of his hold. 'I'll go without the money if necessary.'

'Why are you doing this, Alex?' He sounded almost like a man in shock—he had been that sure of her.

'Doing what?'

'Damn you, Alex,' he swore at the hard insolence now confronting him, 'not ten minutes since you made me feel . . .'

'I *have* to go,' she cut in. She didn't want to hear how he had interpreted her earlier vulnerability. She knew she must have given the impression that he would just have to reach out a hand and take what he wanted.

'Give me one good reason,' he demanded.

Now that he wasn't pushing her, he meant, she couldn't possibly want to leave his island paradise.

'There's someone else,' she lied rashly.

'I don't believe you.' He came back so quickly it appeared his arrogance was unassailable, and then as suddenly, on a harsh driven note, he rasped, 'Who?'

Alex swallowed, wishing she hadn't started this, but pride forced her to go on. 'A young man in England. I promised him I'd be back a long time ago.'

'I see.' His face became a shuttered mask and Alex thought he was accepting her lie very coldly till he shouted down at her, 'No, damn you, Alex Saunders, I don't see!'

And this time as angry as he was when he pulled her into his arms, his kiss sought to devastate with its sensuality, tasting her sweetness, until Alex was clinging to him mindlessly when his hands eventually dragged hers from about his neck and pushed her forcibly from him.

His eyes flicked contemptuously over her wanton loveliness, calling her whore for her response to him while claiming involvement with another man, his kiss a very deliberate, callous attempt to humiliate her and satisfy his arrogant pride. She hated him.

Her head tilted back, her smile insolent. She watched him turn and walk away in disgust, her heart breaking.

She loved him too. Crazy!

CHAPTER ELEVEN

ALEX could have slept till noon and still not had a proper night's rest. As it was, she was woken a little after eight by a maid with a breakfast tray and a message from Andros to be ready in half an hour.

For what, she didn't know—through skipping dinner, she hadn't seen him since yesterday afternoon—but she ate her breakfast on the hop as she washed, dressed in light blue cottons and applied some make-up to cover the faint shadows left by too little sleep and too much crying. The end effect was transforming. She looked bright and lovely, and only a harder glint in her eyes revealed that the sparkle was surface-deep.

For if there had been tears cried, Alex had also done some determined talking to herself. Now, taking the stairs with a firm step, she was almost convinced she had over-dramatised her feelings for Andros, her pride seeming more important to her than pleasing him at any cost. Yesterday she had quite deliberately offended him with her pretence of a fictitious *young* lover. If you loved someone, would you want to hurt them at all?

Certainly she felt rather cool and remote as she walked through the double doors of the lounge and muttered a stiff, 'Yes?' to the man standing at the window with his back to her.

It had him jerking round to face her, then just staring for a long moment with the oddest of expressions—almost as if he didn't know her at all or was taking an imprint to refresh his memory.

Superbly tailored and with his crisp black hair slicked back in perfect order, yet he also looked different. There was a shocking haggardness to the usual well-cut lines of his face, a weariness in the dark eyes that suggested he had slept even less than she had.

What are we doing to each other? Alex thought, as all her careful defences crumbled before Andros Kontos. Whatever he was—amusing and seducing, cruel and corrupting—she loved him. And against having nothing, if he still wanted her, if he said *one* warm word to her, she would meet him halfway—and to hell with her pride.

'Have you packed?' His voice cracked like a pistol shot, freezing the beginnings of a smile on Alex's face.

Hers was the shell-shocked whisper of, 'Not yet.'

'I'll get one of the maids to do it.' He brushed past her like a chilling wind.

There were more words. He would take her to the airport. She was booked on a midday flight to Heathrow. Nicky?—no, she couldn't see Nicky. The boy had already left for school. They would make it a clean break for him. Here was the money he owed her—a cheque for seventeen hundred, and the balance in cash for spending money.

She answered in slow stunned monosyllables when she answered at all. No room to protest. It was the way she'd wanted it. No chance to change her mind. It seemed the way Andros now wanted it too.

Spiro Kallides took them over in the boat, a short respite from those short staccato sentences as she watched the island dwindle on the grey horizon.

A well-trained servant, Spiro did not express the curiosity revealed in his sun-beaten features, but his farewell to the young English girl was kindly, almost concerned, until Andros cut it short with his abruptness.

Then the car journey to Athens and Hellinikon Airport, and more words. She should fasten her seatbelt. Did she want a window open? He'd take the fastest route. Would she like a cigarette? They would be there in little over an hour. On and on, and in between, a heavy silence.

Alex wondered why he talked at all—seated next to her yet seeming too far away to possibly hear her responses. After a while she gave none. The scenery flickered past in a blur of tears. Too fast.

They were there. She brushed her hand over her eyes. She didn't have to—Andros was staring rigidly ahead.

No, she didn't need his help with her bag. Yes, he'd give her love to Nicky. Silence again.

Well, goodbye, and she was scrambling out of the car, grabbing her suitcase from the rear seat, heading for the terminal doors. No glancing back, a voice ordered as she wavered at the entrance and saw the blue limousine reflected in the polished glass. A clean break, the voice urged.

Alex managed to sink on to a seat in the departure lounge before the tears began. They flowed endlessly, and after the first convulsive bout she stopped even trying to stem them. They flowed unheeded down her anguished face as she stifled their noise; they made her invisible.

For an hour people came and went on the bench seat beside her, looked once at the weeping girl and then quickly looked away again—and after a while, her crying became intermittent, the flood became a trickle, leaving only that aching sense of loss.

She had a clown's face—drained of all the sunshine colour and streaked black with mascara. A sad pathetic clown that he watched for ten more minutes, swearing silently before he ended his torture.

'Alex?' he said softly, but the bent head jerked up in a fitful movement and her cry was startled. Then she wouldn't look at him at all as her weeping started again and she covered her face with her hands. It was hardly encouraging, but it embarrassed the old man sitting beside her enough to move on and let Andros slide into his place.

His arm came round her shoulders—a stiff, tentative gesture, but it was enough. Alex didn't ask why he was there. She simply turned her head to his chest, and when his arms gathered her close, curled to him like a soft shivering animal seeking a refuge till its fright went away. With his strength and warmth, he gave it, until she was at last calm and quiet, and able to face the world again.

Andros lit them both cigarettes, and leaning her head back on the pillar behind her, she dragged deeply on hers. She sensed him scrutinising her ravaged face and waited for him to speak, but he appeared to have run out of words since she had last seen him. She was glad in one way—any more cold impersonalities would have been unbearable after the tender way he had just comforted her—but they had to speak some time.

Out of sheer nervousness she muttered, 'I must look a fright.' His laugh was low but only slightly mocking.

'That bad, eh?' she quizzed nervously, as she recalled the dark eye make-up that must be streaking her cheeks.

Andros shook his head. 'I've never heard you say something so . . . feminine before about your looks,' he explained his humour. 'You look fine,' he reassured her dutifully.

Alex slanted him a sideways glance. 'Honestly?'

'No,' he admitted with a rueful smile and she managed a half-smile in return, but it faded quickly. 'It is Nicky, yes?' he asked carefully.

Slowly she nodded, unprepared to reveal his share of her tears. Lowering her eyes back to her lap, she did, however, make an attempt at correcting one false idea, with considerable effect.

'You think I just dumped him in that orphanage, but I didn't. I love Nicky as if he were my own . . .'

'I know that,' he inserted quietly.

'. . . And I was jobless and homeless,' she rushed on, 'so they took him away from me. But I would . . .'

This time Alex interrupted herself as the echo of her previous impulsive words began to resound deafeningly in her head. 'As if he were my own', she'd said—quite clearly and emphatically.

Even before she raised her eyes back to his, she found it difficult to believe his calm reply had meant he had missed her slip altogether, but somehow impossible when she met his dark intelligent stare.

He knew!

Cold with reaction, her mind flitted with a rush of fragmented memories, snatches of conversation, which together made an awful sense that had her feeling she had been painfully, staggeringly dense all these weeks ... How many weeks?

'How long?' she asked aloud, and despite the absence of any explanation, he understood her instantly.

'I received a report on you and your sister three weeks after your arrival in Greece,' he sighed.

'Before I tried to tell you?'

'Yes.' Andros's dark brows drew together. He could rarely predict quite how she would react to anything, but her calmness now seemed ominous.

In fact Alex was gripped by waves of shock as she marked events before and after his awareness of her deception, placing their night stroll on the beach on the 'after' side. Why had he kept silent long after Nicky's custody was guaranteed to him?—Why else but to torment her!

'At the risk of inviting hysterics, Alex, could you possibly say something more?' His voice intruded with less than its normal assurance.

Alex stood up, shaking with anger and hurt, to deliver, 'You're quite a bastard, aren't you?' before she made her move.

He was still thinking about it while she walked away towards the main hall of the airport.

'Damn you, Alex!' he shouted incredulously.' You haven't the nerve to be mad at me?' Hurrying after her, he forcibly intercepted her path and yanked her round to face him. 'We both played the same game—lying by omission. At least *I* forgave you for it!'

For a few seconds Alex simply stared at him, not believing what she had heard. Maybe she had him convinced she was tough enough not to be destroyed by his 'games'. And yes, perhaps, he had felt her deception deserved punishment. But that he would *dare* to say that . . . that he'd forgiven her for it!

'You *forgave* me!' she repeated, dropping her suitcase with a carelessness that almost landed it on his foot. As he swore again, Alex was sorry she hadn't taken more care and placed it squarely on target. Getting some control over her fury, she accused bitterly, 'Don't you mean you spent each and every minute since you discovered your evil-minded assumptions about me were wrong, working on paying me back for letting *you* make a fool of *yourself*?'

'All right, Alex, that's enough!' he interrupted, giving her a small punishing shake. 'I did have some pretty wild ideas at the beginning that just might have given you reason to lie. Perhaps I've kept quiet too long. But don't jump to conclusions as to why.'

'Oh, come on!' Alex flared at the stern warning, now also oblivious of their surroundings, 'I was meant to fall for that macho Greek charm—so slow and sure, and all the time, all those weeks, really so cold and calculating. And if I'd let you make love to me that would have justified your warped imaginings.'

'*My* warped imaginings!' he erupted, the hand on her arm almost jerking her off her feet as it brought her nearer his furious face. 'Compared with yours, Alex Saunders . . .'

'Stop pretending! Just because I didn't play along with . . .'

A harsh laugh cut her short. 'Oh, you didn't play along, did you?'

'No, I . . .' she began, but was overruled by his low accusing jeer.

'Well, *I* seem to remember a girl on a moonlit beach moaning so sweetly she nearly drove me crazy when she tired of *her* teasing game . . .'

'I wasn't . . .'

'Or a girl on a hillside playing *me* along so well she had me thinking I could have had her right there as she twisted round me like . . .'

Andros's head jerked backwards in stunned surprise at the sheer force of Alex's slap. It had been an act of desperation, a last resort to silence his mockery of her weakness for him, but perhaps it was a fitting way to end things—full circle back to that first violent meeting in the park.

Only as she took a stumbling step backwards and stared at him in horrified fascination, Alex realised that this time the rage constricting his features wasn't going to be controlled. This time ... she shut her eyes in an attitude of prayer and waited for that thunderous anger to reach out and strike her.

Then suddenly a voice invaded their little island of hostility. As intervention, it was scarcely divine, but it did save Alex from the slap Andros fully intended to return, for they both froze and listened to the message being repeated over the airport loudspeakers, now in English,

'Would Mr Andros Kontos or Miss Alex Saunders please report to the information desk.'

'Nicky!' It was a joint exclamation before they raced together to the desk at the far end of the hall.

'What's wrong?' Alex appealed, her brain refusing to make sense of Andros's hurried exchange with the airport official who whisked them through to a private office, but he was already speaking into the telephone. At first he talked rapidly, and then more slowly, repeating the same instruction several times.

Alex had translated it as, 'In Greek, Mario,' before he finally handed the receiver to her, saying, 'It's Mario. Something's wrong with Nicky, but I can't understand what.'

It was small wonder, because the young man on the other end of the line was highly excited and had abandoned his second language to revert to a garbled Italian even Alex had a problem deciphering. But she caught 'boy' and 'very sick' and for long seconds a liberal share of Mario's evident panic.

Face pale, she swayed slightly, to be steadied by Andros's hand at her waist. 'Alex, what's happening?'

'I'm ... I'm not sure,' she mumbled faintly, but seeing all her anxiety mirrored in his eyes, she strove to keep calm. Cutting into Mario's ramblings, she took command of the conversation in crisp tones, and while establishing what was going on, she relayed piecemeal to the man beside her, 'Nicky had a stomach upset at school ... Mario was fetched to take him home ... he decided to take him up to the villa and then telephone the island ... Nicky wasn't too ill until Mario told him ...'

Frowning, Alex chose not to translate further, but Andros did it for her with a heavy undertone of, 'You were no longer there.' She could not deny it.

Asking Mario to wait, she revealed the rest. 'He's having an asthma attack. He should have his inhaler on him, but Mario says he can't find it.'

'Has he summoned a doctor?' Andros pressed, and at her nod, instructed finally, 'Tell him to inform Nicky that you're coming home as soon as possible.'

'But ...'

'Just tell him, Alex,' he urged, and after she had, she was grabbed by the hand, swept alongside him out of the airport buildings across to the car park and installed back in the Mercedes.

She didn't argue, not even to point out that they had left her suitcase behind. Indeed she didn't say anything the whole journey back, and all Andros's concentration was given over to getting them to the villa with a speed that would have been alarming if her fears for Nicky hadn't superseded everything. She simply clung on to the edge of her seat and tortured herself by imagining the worst if Nicky's asthma attack couldn't be contained.

Yet when they eventually drew up between Mario's battered Skoda and the doctor's sleeker BMW and hurried to the set of shutters open on the upper balcony, even Alex's experience of illness left her unprepared for the sight of Nicky, oxygen mask strapped over his mouth and clearly beyond consciousness.

While a distracted Andros flew to the bedside, it was to her the doctor directed his comments, and it was left to a visibly calmer Mario to confirm that the Greek was telling her that the danger was passed: that Nicky, now under mild sedation, would soon require no more oxygen but simply rest for the slight virus that had initially sent him home from school.

Andros, seemingly oblivious of all else, continued to hold Nicky's hand, even when the doctor removed the mask, checked his patient's pulse with a murmur of satisfaction, and made ready to leave.

With Mario still acting as translator, they walked along the balcony, while the doctor stressed that the boy's 'father' had no reason to worry. He would call again in the morning, but purely to set their minds at ease. In the meantime, his 'mother' looked pale and exhausted herself, and would benefit from some rest. Alex smiled wanly, shaking her head when Mario asked whether he should explain that Andros was not the child's father. It didn't seem that important any more whose child Nicky was, as long as he was all right.

Returning to the bedroom, nothing had changed. Still facing Nicky, Andros's profile was a fixed mask, more like a perfect Greek statue than the first occasion Alex had seen him. But now she knew that below that rigid exterior, he was a man of deep emotion, and if it was merely passion he offered her, to the boy it was a fierce protective love. She felt envious of it, shut out by it—forgotten and alone.

Eventually Mario became embarrassed on Alex's behalf and, mumbling an excuse that Lucia would want to know how things stood, he went downstairs to telephone.

'Andros . . .' she came closer and pressed softly for his attention, 'Andros, he's going to be fine.'

At last he turned his head in her direction, and she repeated more firmly the reassurances the doctor had given. For long seconds his dark intense gaze was focused completely on her, and for a moment as he rose from the bed, she imagined he was going to hold out his arms for her—and she would have flown into them, to comfort and be comforted. But apparently he had not forgotten the way things were between them.

'You must never do that again, Alex.' The words were spoken quietly but with a chilling air of finality.

Do what? Alex would have asked. He couldn't mean *never leave*! That wasn't possible. But he didn't give her the chance to ask, for he swept past her to the door, as though the room's atmosphere was suddenly unbearable to him.

A confused Alex sank down on a bedside chair to wait for Nicky to come round. Already his colour was improved, his breathing steady and relaxed. His hand was warm from the man's as she clasped it gently in hers. Panic over, reaction set in: she began to cry softly again and after the tears, she too fell asleep, so weary she did not wake on being moved.

And if her dreaming was disturbed at one point, it was by the pleasantest of sounds—Nicky's voice brightly responding to a deeper masculine tone—and when she woke as the day drifted into evening shadows, it was to find herself lying on the bed she had once used in the villa and Andros in the chair next to her, cradling a sleeping Nicky in his arms. The simple image was wholly moving until the complexity of their situation intruded.

'Is he . . .'

'Fine,' she was reassured quietly. 'He was awake earlier and needed to see for himself that you were back. It was easier to take him to you.'

She didn't ask how she'd ended up here. It was obvious. Vexed, she said, 'You should have woken me. I wanted to explain things to him.'

'Don't worry. I've done so,' Andros told her, but, if anything, it served to increase Alex's anxiety when she recalled his earlier strangeness. Again he frustrated her desire to question him as he stood up, carefully bracing the child's weight. 'I'll put Nicky back to bed. He'll

probably sleep the night through. Why don't you have
a shower while I make something for us to eat?' he
suggested calmly.

Too calmly, Alex judged, as she sat upright against
the bedrest after he had left. Or perhaps not so much
calmly as decisively. She remembered him in this mood
from other occasions: that first night in the villa when
he had dictated his 'compromise'; her initial attempt to
leave the island he had summarily overruled. It made
her nervous, especially as she found herself floundering
for any real determination of her own.

After a shower she did feel livelier, better ready for
battle if it came down to that, although she wished she
was more appropriately dressed for it. Discarding the
crumpled clothes she had slept in and having no others,
she had to resort to one of his shirts and the silky briefs
she'd discovered on her last stay. The outfit was as
respectable as a mini-dress, for the blue shirt had a long
tail that almost reached her knees, but Alex felt a rather
comic figure in its bagginess.

She suspected she probably was, because he stared at
her oddly when she made an entrance in the living
room. He was setting the table in the dining area in
front of the window as she hastily excused, 'I had to
borrow one of your shirts. We left my suitcase at the
airport.'

'It's all right, we'll get you some clothes tomorrow,'
he returned with a suspiciously satisfied smile, and
ignored her comment that it would be simpler to
retrieve her case. He did, however, reply to her
mutinous look with a dry, 'Let's eat first.'

Well, Alex thought as she tucked into the delicious
steak he had prepared, at least they were in agreement
over something: any serious discussion of the future was
bound to end in argument. Tacitly they both avoided
anything remotely controversial while they compensated
for a missed lunch. In fact after Alex did her small part
by making coffee, Andros made it plain he had no wish
to argue.

'First I would like you to believe I had no great plan of revenge in keeping silent. It was, in retrospect, perhaps a foolish thing to do, but round you, Alex, one tends to act on impulse,' he began, but if there was any mockery intended, it seemed directed at himself. 'At the time I felt I needed some advantages.'

'Very well,' Alex accepted, although not quite following the last. 'And I'm sorry I told all those lies, but you were being . . .'

'Impossible?' Andros supplied with a wry smile when Alex, for once, exercised some tact. 'I must admit I am not used to opposition. You came as something of a . . . surprise.'

Alex didn't risk asking which kind, even if he did sound amused. She still had the impression he was leading to some point she wouldn't like.

Indeed he quickly reverted to seriousness with, 'I also regret the injustice I did you and your sister with my cynical misreading of the situation. But whatever else, I realised very early that your devotion to the boy is real. And that is why I have always found it difficult to believe you'd leave him behind.'

Deliberately or not, he made Alex feel she was abandoning the child. 'I can't compete with the sort of home you can provide. Nicky accepted that I'd have to leave some day—I explained it to him again and he understood. And *he wants* to stay in Greece,' she defended her actions.

'Without you?—I don't think so. And you can't either, not after today,' Andros insisted, holding up a silencing hand when Alex would have spoken. 'You may have prepared the boy, and perhaps I'm to blame for today by not allowing you to say goodbye to him, but he had ceased believing you would be leaving. He thought you were happy,' he finished on an accusing note.

Had she appeared so to Nicky? She supposed she must have in the latter part of the summer; she supposed she had been during all those long days spent cruising the islands, until she had realised just who had made them special for her.

'It was for Nicky's sake you came back to the airport.' Alex wasn't sure if it was a question or statement on her part, but she took his shrug to mean his reason was irrelevant, before he crushed out his cigarette and leaned forward suddenly to place his hand on hers.

'Look, Alex, you can see how it is. It doesn't matter that you're not his mother. The boy adores you—he thinks the sun and moon rise on you. You can't leave us like this.' His tone was demanding, and yet his eyes were asking—a strange mixture of arrogance and tenderness. Again Alex envied Nicky this man's love.

'I don't think I should stay longer,' she murmured, trying to say it with conviction.

Ignoring her words, he enclosed her hand with a warm strength. 'You want to be with Nicky. Come back, Alex—your terms. For a while at least. He'll wait—I would.'

Alex almost gave herself away by saying, 'Who?' and then frowned, remembering in time her invention of the young man anxious for her return.

'There isn't . . .' she intended rescinding that last rash lie, but she wasn't allowed to finish before Andros pressed on.

'If not to the island, then here. Or Athens if you prefer the city. Not the penthouse—I'll buy a house.'

'You'd do that?' said Alex, astounded.

'I am a rich man,' he discounted the extravagance of another house, and reading the doubt in Alex's expression, intensified his persuasions. 'Wherever you want to live, Alex. And anything you want to do—work as a translator or study at the university—I can fix it . . . anything! I can give you so much more than that young man back in England, I know I can.'

If Alex had been hesitating, it was at the temptation to do exactly what she wanted—be with Nicky *and* Andros. But his last words acted as a sobering reminder of why she had rejected him with that lie just a day ago. And if now he was pleading on Nicky's behalf, she wasn't so naïve as to think it wouldn't end up how she had imagined—with Andros avoiding commitment by buying his pleasure from her until they both could do without her, and she—the fool—she was ready to give herself, body and soul, for nothing.

'No, I can't!' she exclaimed, and almost knocked over her chair, wresting her hand from his grip. 'And I won't talk about it any more.'

'Alex, where are you going?' Andros demanded, more surprised than anything at her sudden flight.

'To my room,' she threw over her shoulder, already at the door, and was through it and up the stairs before he could say anything that would weaken her resolve.

She did not, however, count on his, and when she turned from switching on her bedside lamp, she would have cried out in fright, if the man who had followed her so quietly, hadn't warned, 'Don't wake the boy!'

'Then get out of here!' Alex hissed back.

'After we've finished our discussion,' he said, anger behind the muted tone as he pushed away from the door.

'We have. I said no, remember?'

'I'm trying to be reasonable,' he muttered heavily at Alex's air of insolence.

'Are you?' She didn't see it that way. Straining to keep her voice down, she countered, 'Your idea of being reasonable, Andros, is telling someone what you've decided, and then expecting them to fall in with it.'

'I gave you alternatives,' he pointed out, eyes hardening on her as he approached. When she made to avoid him, he grabbed her, almost growling in his demand, 'What other choices can I offer?'

And she was being ungrateful, Alex interpreted his attitude, retaliating, 'Well, forgive me if I'm being unco-operative, but—first a bribe to leave, now a bribe to stay?'

'Bribe?' He frowned darkly.

'You can give me *so much more* than my young man,' she echoed in a derisive tone, failing to twist free of his hold.

'I didn't mean money,' he ground out.

'No?' A single word, but it breathed scepticism.

'Not entirely.'

'What else?' she challenged scornfully.

'Damn you, Alex, don't tease. You know what I mean!' he accused before his temper snapped altogether.

The only warning Alex had was his cool breath fleetingly on her cheek, and then his mouth fastened on hers, forcing her lips to part for a total invasion that stifled sound and reason. She couldn't move her head, could scarcely struggle, as one hand braced the back of her skull, the other angled against her spine to clasp her body with a rough sensuality. But the scream locked inside her throat against the sudden assault died first to a loud whimper as his kiss failed to meet brutality, and then became a deep moan as it began to stir that wanton hunger for him. Once more the girl on the beach, the girl on the hillside—breathless and clinging.

'You know what I want,' he said, his soft taunt brushing against her cheek when his mouth grazed away from hers with a satisfied groan. 'And you want it too. Say it, Alex,' he urged, his hand caressing to draw a shivering response.

'And if I say no—no, I don't?' she breathed, conscious of her vulnerability and needing to know she had the choice.

'Then I'd say you were lying,' he returned, but Alex didn't disclaim it, because the words were punctuated by small tasting kisses on the arch of her neck, and were as tender as his following, 'But I'd forgive you for it as I've always done—every hurting word, every cutting look, every silly lie—and only wish I could be cool and calculating about wanting you.'

It was a low seductive murmur now, curling round

her senses in the half-light, and Alex felt sure if she said anything in reply, it would betray the unwilling love for him that governed her erratic behaviour. And somehow it seemed the most guilty secret of all. But when Andros suddenly set her from him, his deep groan could have come from her dry throat.

'Andros?' she heard her own desperation as she sensed him poised to leave.

'We'll talk tomorrow. I'll leave you alone,' he promised, his voice thick with frustration, believing her silence another rejection.

'Andros!' This time it was an impulsive cry as he reached the door.

He wheeled round on a plea of, 'For God's sake, Alex, don't make it like this!'

'I'm not . . .' she couldn't seem to find words for her feelings, but she had no doubt of them. Perhaps she had no pride left if she loved him enough to accept what little he offered—his 'wanting'. But, terrified this moment would never come again, she had to do something!

She'd die of embarrassment if he despised her for it, she swore silently, as she tried to compensate for her verbal inadequacy and her total ignorance of what a mature sophisticated man might expect.

'What the devil . . .' Andros bit off on a soft curse to stare hypnotised by what Alex was doing—her fingers having already shakily started to unfasten the buttons of her borrowed shirt.

When she finished to stand in the soft light, naked above the silky briefs covering her hips and her breasts full and erect to the male eyes on them, an acutely shy Alex couldn't even look in his direction. Sensing his gaze moving over her flushed skin, she was torn between a desire to dive for cover and a hunger to feel more than his eyes upon her.

'I can't . . .' She tried to tell him her nerveless fingers refused to go any further, and indeed if he hesitated any longer her courage would give way altogether.

Perhaps he understood, for one second he was a tall looming shadow and the next, a warm vibrant force enclosing her shivering frame with a body that seemed to be trembling as badly as hers.

'You'd better not be teasing,' he said, a hoarse appeal as he hugged her tightly, possessively for a long moment before leading her to the bed.

Secure in his arms, Alex felt instantly nervous when he left her to discard his own clothing with what sounded like a careless haste. What if he expected her to know much more than she did? She had given him the impression of experience. How could she begin to please him? She still couldn't even look at him.

When his arms reached out to gather her close for the shock of his bare skin against hers, her eyes did widen momentarily at the sight of the dark handsome head lowering towards hers before his fingers threaded in her hair and his mouth claimed hers in a sweet drugging kiss.

'Lie still,' he ordered softly, as stroking hands on the swell of her breasts were replaced with demanding lips that first unnerved her with the sudden spasm of desire they sent shuddering through her body.

But when his mouth continued to bite and play, Alex gradually lost her fears and inhibitions to excite him in return: with her small moaning sighs of desire; the upward curve of her body against his; the urging caress of her hands on his smooth muscular back.

His breathing more ragged, the hand splayed motionless against her stomach became impatient with the remainder of her clothing, slipping down to touch her with an intimacy that drew a startled sob from her throat and then left her defenceless, naked to his gaze.

Words weren't needed to tell her he found her beautiful when his eyes feasted openly on the sight of her against his dark sheets, skin a honey gold save where the sun hadn't touched it. Alex made to cover her nakedness, but he pulled the covering away altogether, with a deep growling laugh as her lashes swept down to shield her eyes.

Slowly his hands spread over the flat of her stomach upwards once more to lovingly cup her breasts, to tease her with his knowing fingers while his mouth came down on hers to smother her small cries of delight, until she was clinging to him, arching against him, aching for him. Mindless with pleasure already given, if she had been capable of thought at all, Alex would have believed herself immune to pain.

She wasn't. It came in one sharp burst that first caused a loud whimper of fright and surprise, then flung her eyes open to meet the stunned glaze of his before she buried her head in his shoulder to hear his throaty, loving acceptance of, 'Crazy, beautiful girl.'

Overwhelmed by love for him, she ignored any pain to move against him invitingly, was soothed and then roused once more by the slow, controlled urge of his lovemaking, was dazed and delirious when his fulfilment came in a hoarse cry of her name.

But afterwards, when his breathing quietened and they lay side by side, Alex wished she could slink away or hide under the bedclothes from the wondering question she read in his expression, and was more child than woman when she whispered, 'I don't want to talk about it—please, Andros?'

The anguished plea in her eyes was answered by an indulgence in his and the light brush of his fingers against her cheek.

'Later, then,' he allowed, reaching out for her. 'Let me hold you now.'

And Alex, lying cradled in his arms, head pillowed in the curve of his shoulder and believing sleep would be impossible with him near, drifted from consciousness on a tiny flame of hope.

When next her eyes flickered open, it was to a blaze of autumn sunshine filling the room and the sight of the man now her lover sitting at the edge of the bed looking down at her. Already showered and clean-shaven, he was immaculately dressed in a dark blue bathrobe while she was ... realising exactly what she was, Alex grabbed for the sheet twisted round her waist, blushing furiously at his soft laugh.

'Beautiful, shy virgin,' he murmured, but didn't stop her hiding her nudity. 'You should have told me, Alex. I might have hurt you badly, I wanted you so much.'

'It doesn't matter,' she dismissed, for if his mixture of gentleness and passion had allowed her to imagine he cared for her in any special way, the fragment of a dream had been quickly torn away by his 'wanted'.

'I'd rather hoped it might,' he said in the same deeply serious tones, and stretched out a hand to tilt her chin so she was forced to look at him. There were faint shadows under her eyes, a fuller swelling to her lips, but the night had not erased the look of a girl rather than a woman. 'When I held you sleeping next to my heart, I began to believe I had received a very precious gift, more precious than just the taking of your innocence. Was I wrong in my conceit?'

A speech as pretty as any man could have made to ask a woman if she loved him, and Alex felt her enraptured look must be betraying it. Half forgetting he had asked her a question, she smiled, moved between wonder and joy and laughter, but now *Andros* needed the words.

'I swear if I didn't *love* you so much, Alex Saunders,' he half snarled, half laughed at her silence, 'I'd beat an answer out of you. Now, yes or no?'

'No! No, you weren't wrong,' she almost shouted it.

Did he say he loved her? For a moment it seemed magical as she was held enchanted in his warm, loving arms.

'Perhaps I shall beat you anyway,' Andros smiled, laying her back against the pillows to gaze at her, 'After we're married.'

'Married?'

'As quickly as possible, I think,' he passed over her startled question, and lowering his eyes to her slim body, added, meaningfully, 'Just in case.'

Alex missed the smile in those eyes.

'Andros, we can't ...' she trailed off, struggling between an impulse for once not to question his arrogance and an intelligence that warned her to be cautious.

'That's not a good enough reason to marry,' she declared eventually, and deepened his frown by quoting him, 'that I was too stupid or too cunning to take precautions.'

'You're not very good at forgiving or trusting, are you, Alex Saunders? Give me your hand!' he instructed briskly, but took it before it could even be offered to him. 'Now say yes.'

'Yes? To what? she quizzed.

'This.' Not giving her the option to resist, Andros slipped the ring he drew out of his robe pocket on to her finger. 'And if you imagine my having an engagement ring on me is coincidence, you're definitely crazy!'

Perhaps they both were, Alex considered as she stared bemusedly at the diamond-encrusted sapphire now adorning her left hand, a beautiful ring that flashed a deep blue light.

'If you don't like it, we'll get you another. I brought it back from Italy, a token, in the hope that you might feel the way I did,' Andros continued, closing her hand with his. 'Only I never got the chance to ask you. I took you to the airport because I didn't want to protract the agony, but I just couldn't stop myself from going back. Was he important to you—this young man in England?'

Appalled by the way she had misunderstood him, Alex shook her head and admitted sheepishly, 'Actually, I made him up.' At his mixed look of exasperation and relief she explained, 'I thought you were on the point of asking me to have an affair and I wasn't prepared to compromise then ... but I am now ... I think ... you don't have to ...'

'I *want* to,' he cut in emphatically. 'I love you, Alex, *I'm* not willing to compromise—and you've already said yes.'

Had she? Alex had no recollection of it. She had a feeling she was going to find herself married to him no matter what she said.

Still she tried to be sensible. 'But marriage might be the bigger compromise, don't you see? Even if some miracle could turn me into the right sort of wife for a Greek tycoon, I don't think I'd like to be her.'

'And I wouldn't want you to be,' he responded without hesitation, but it didn't clear Alex's frown of insecurity. With a touch of wryness, Andros set out to convince her, saying, 'When I was a young man, my father made the usual speech about there being two types of women—the kind to be enjoyed through the advantages of wealth and the kind he and my mother regularly produced as suitable wife material. Well, I can't deny taking part of his advice, but I never met any of his "nice" Greek girls I couldn't live without. And then along came a young English girl who's not in any category. She's amusing and irritating, clever and crazy, shy and impudent, totally contradictory. Whatever—I love *her*,' he stressed, cupping the side of her face with his hand.

'And I love you,' Alex said very quietly, almost shyly, and then, needing to be sure he understood, 'I wasn't teasing you before. I just didn't . . .'

Recalling her former boldness, Andros had to smile at her reluctance to put things into words. 'I realise that now. At the time I thought you must know how I felt about you. And last night *I* really meant that I could look after you better, love you more, than any other man. I warn you, I'm going to be a very jealous husband,' he finished.

'Andros, do you think we should be so impulsive?' Alex persisted anxiously.

But apparently Andros had concluded that enough talking had been done, because suddenly he began to pull gently on her covering.

'Andros, I don't think . . .' she broke off, the rest lost on a sigh.

'You don't have to,' he murmured against the tautness of the breast he had exposed, his caressing lips already making it near impossible for Alex to think much anyway. Then with a return of his arrogance he lifted his head away to assert, 'I love you. You love me. That will be enough.'

'Will it?' Alex wanted to believe, but she was too used to the impermanence of relationships. 'For how long, Andros?'

His black brows knitted in an aggressive line as he replaced the sheet over her. 'This isn't going to be any modern, temporary marriage, Alex, and you'd better understand that.'

His sober announcement made it sound like a life sentence, but he relented at the beginnings of a smile on Alex's face, clearing doubts, telling him that was the way she wanted it to be.

'As soon as possible, yes?' This time he was asking and now Alex drew confidence from his urgency, but before she could respond to it, they spotted the small figure hesitating in the doorway.

Unembarrassed, Andros waved him inside, and Nicky obviously found nothing odd about the situation, for he nestled on his uncle's lap and got right to the point.

'Is she coming back?'

'Why don't you ask her?' Andros suggested to the dark head tilted to his.

'Are you coming home, Lex?' Nicky repeated the vital question and if Alex, looking between man and boy and seeing the same grave appeal in their eyes, knew herself the victim of a conspiracy, it was a loving one.

And days later when they returned to the island, Alex wearing the other ring Andros had given her, that was how it felt.

She was coming home.

Coming Next Month in Harlequin Presents!

751 DARK TYRANT Helen Blanchin
A young Australian discovers that her stepfather used her as collateral for a loan. Now he's dead. Payment is due—in full. And she's supposed to be thankful that her blackmailer intends to marry her.

752 LETTER FROM BRONZE MOUNTAIN Rosemary Carter
Love at first sight betrays a South African artist when the man she meets and loses her heart to turns out to be the man she holds responsible for her sister's death.

753 AN INDEPENDENT WOMAN Claire Harrison
In the clear light of the Canadian Rockies, a sensitive woman is challenged by a forceful man to go with him to the prairies...to find out who she really is.

754 INTIMATE Donna Huxley
Things go from bad to worse when an unscrupulous executive hounds a young computer researcher out of the firm and out of the job market. But surely the man in her life won't believe the lies!

755 RULES OF THE GAME Penny Jordan
Beginner's luck doesn't hold up for an English photographer posing as her flamboyantly beautiful cousin when she's disqualified for cheating by the man who wrote the rules for the game of love.

756 THE OPEN MARRIAGE Flora Kidd
An English furniture designer still loves her Welsh husband, even though she left him once she learned about the other woman in his life. But before she initiates divorce proceedings....

757 UNTAMED Carole Mortimer
A young, publicity-shy woman attracts the unwanted attentions of an actor who gives a brilliant portrayal of a man in love. If only she could believe him.

758 TOO FAR, TOO FAST Elizabeth Oldfield
They meet again in Hong Kong and seem fated to sacrifice love a second time for the sake of his professional tennis career. Then they discover the manipulations of a real pro.